Relentless Havoc

Relentless Havoc

Montana Mayhem
Book 5

Millie Copper

Written by Millie Copper

Edited by Ameryn Tucker

Proofread by MDC Proofreading and WMH Cheryl

Cover design by Dauntless Cover Design

Also by Millie Copper

Montana Mayhem Series

Unending Havoc: Montana Mayhem Book 1

Ruthless Havoc: Montana Mayhem Book 2

Merciless Havoc: Montana Mayhem Book 3

Cruel Havoc: Montana Mayhem Book 4

Havoc in Wyoming Series

Wyoming Refuge: A Havoc in Wyoming Prequel

Havoc in Wyoming: Part 1, Caldwell's Homestead

Havoc in Wyoming: Part 2, Katie's Journey

Havoc in Wyoming: Part 3, Mollie's Quest

Havoc Begins: A Havoc in Wyoming Story

Havoc in Wyoming: Part 4, Shields and Ramparts

Havoc in Wyoming: Part 5, Fowler's Snare

Havoc Rises: A Havoc in Wyoming Story

Havoc in Wyoming: Part 6, Pestilence in the Darkness

Christmas on the Mountain: A Havoc in Wyoming Novella

Havoc Peaks: A Havoc in Wyoming Story

Havoc in Wyoming: Part 7, My Refuge and Fortress

Nonfiction Books

Sourdough for Your Food Storage: Add Nutrition and Variety to Your Baked Goods

Sprouts for Your Food Storage: Add Nutrition and Variety to Your Diet

Stretchy Beans: Nutritious, Economical Meals the Easy Way

Stock the Real Food Pantry: A Handbook for Making the Most of Your Pantry

Design a Dish: Save Your Food Dollars

Real Food Hits the Road: Budget Friendly Tips, Ideas, and Recipes for Enjoying Real Food Away from Home

Join My Reader's Club!

Receive a complimentary copy of *Wicked Havoc: A Montana Mayhem Prequel.* As part of my reader's club, you'll be the first to know about new releases and specials. I also share info on books I'm reading, preparedness tips, and more. Please sign up at:

MillieCopper.com/Wicked

Chapter 1

Kimba
Thursday, August 6

I lean against the heavy entrance timber, resting my rifle. *Get it together, Kimba. Focus only on what is happening. They need you.*

The tingling starts in my hands. My throat tightens. *Focus, focus. Breathe in through your nose . . . one, two, three, four. Hold the breath . . . one, two, three, four. Out through your mouth . . . one, two, three, four.*

What used to be so simple, easy even, is now a colossal struggle. Rey, my husband of eighteen years, is walking into danger. I'm his overwatch; it's my job to protect him.

But I don't want to be here. *Slow breath in . . .*

What once sounded like such a wonderful plan, a patriotic endeavor, is meaningless. We were fooling ourselves to think we could make a difference. *Hold the breath . . .*

I was fooling myself.

I tried before, tried to make a difference. That ended badly. People were hurt. People died. But this time . . . my son—my baby. *Ach. Forget the stupid box breathing. It no longer helps anyway.*

We could've stayed there—could've stayed where we buried him, set up a long-term camp, and waited it out. Even better, we could've never started this stupid journey in the first place. We had safety and friendship, family even, at the ski lodge.

Now here we are, in danger again. My two daughters are hiding out, waiting to see if their parents get themselves killed. At seventeen, Nicole's old enough to take care of her little sister, but she shouldn't be saddled with an eight-year-old because of stupidity.

They shouldn't be in this position.

Nicole should be excited about her final year of high school, taking senior pictures, planning for college . . . maybe even getting her heart broken by her first true love.

Naomi should be playing at the park with her friends, doing cartwheels in the grass, laughing and being carefree. Instead, they're holed up in a ditch in what has become a third world country.

The United States we knew is no more. The happiness we knew is gone, snuffed out forever.

Atticus, the young man with Rey, lifts a hand to signal *stop* when they reach the halfway point between the entrance of the sprawling ranch and the main house. He cups his hands around his mouth. "Scott? It's Atticus Dosen. Scott Pierce? You there?"

Atticus's voice rings strong and true. Determined.

When I met him just over a year ago, he was slightly chubby, not yet eighteen, and mourning the recent loss of his father. Today, not only is he physically sculpted but he's a strong leader. Even with the death of his mom a mere few hours ago, his determination doesn't falter.

He calls out again before a faint voice responds. "Atticus? Wow! I can't believe you're here."

Standing next to me, Axel Dosen, younger brother to Atticus, mutters something and then steps out from behind our cover.

"Wait!" I reach out my arm to stop him. "Wait until Rey gives the all-clear sign."

Shamefaced, he steps behind the heavy timbers. "Sorry. Wasn't thinking."

I direct my attention back to Rey and Atticus. A tall, heavy framed man steps from the house.

"That's Scott," Axel whispers. "He's worked for us since I was in fourth grade—about six years. He looks good."

I give a nod. Living on this cattle ranch must provide superior food to what we've had. I self-consciously look at my own waistline. The couple of years before the attacks, I seemed to be fighting a losing battle with the scale. Spinning three times a week, weightlifting two, and Pilates at least once weren't enough to keep the pounds away.

Turns out, forced rations and the need to survive is the perfect diet for someone in her forties. Who knew?

On the heels of the man is a woman—a girl maybe—at least a foot shorter. They meet up with Rey and Atticus and talk for a few moments before my husband turns and motions for us to join them.

I close my eyes and let out a long eight-count breath, feeling the tension drain from me.

From the timbers across the driveway, Victoria Dawson, one of my traveling companions, asks, "Should I get the others?"

Standing next to her, her oldest son Brett says, "I'll get them."

I hold up my hand. "Wait. Just wait."

Chapter 2

Nicole

"N'cole?" Little LJ tugs at my sleeve.

"Shh." I put my finger to my lips. "We're hiding, remember?"

He lifts a shoulder in response. "Trish pooped her pants. I smell it."

I look to Patti, mom to both three-year-old LJ and baby Trish. She gives a slight nod before setting down her rifle.

My younger sister, Naomi, is sitting with Trish on the blanket and asks if Patti needs help.

Patti shakes her head.

"We'll keep watch." My voice is low, barely audible as I motion to Jameson Dawson. We're waiting—*hiding*—while my mom and dad, along with the rest of our group, find out if the Dosen farmhouse is safe. We've been traveling for months to get here, and now that we are . . . I stifle a sigh.

The Dosen ranch—or Double D, as the ranch and its brand are officially known—is home to Atticus and Axel, the only surviving members of their family.

Their mom, Jennifer, whose body is on a homemade travois next to me, died when we reached the small town of Simms. A bear attacked her last night, dragging her out of her tent and mauling her. There's a deep ache in my heart. I miss her already. I still miss her son Asher, twin to Atticus, who died a few months back in an explosion.

And I really miss my younger brother, Nate, who was killed in a freak tornado six weeks ago.

Nate.

The pain of his death is still strong. Bitter. He had barely even made it to his teen years. His death changed everything. My mom and dad, who used to be so in love, so devoted, can barely even look at each other now.

Mom especially. She tries to hide it, tries to pretend like she doesn't blame my dad for Nate dying, but it's still there. The occasions she does look at Dad, it's with narrowed eyes. And I notice the way she stiffens or moves away when he touches her, or how she talks to him, to most of us, in a snippy tone.

I've tried to be understanding, to know she's hurting, grieving. But we all are. All of us loved Nate. We hadn't yet recovered from losing Asher when Nate died. And now Jennifer's dead too.

It's exhausting. Moving through our days, waiting for the other shoe to drop, for someone else to be hurt or killed . . .

I clench my teeth as I anticipate the gunfire in response to the rest of our group approaching the Dosen ranch. Nothing else has gone as expected on this trip, so it makes sense we'll have to fight for the brothers' ranch.

"You okay?" Jameson asks.

I clench my jaw. "Fine."

"Really? Because I'm not. I hate all of this."

Jameson has been a thorn in my side since before we left the ski lodge in March. He's a know-it-all who doesn't know Jack.

Even when we were still living at the lodge and were training on how to use our backcountry splitboards—special snowboards that separate to be used as cross-country skis, then go back together for riding—he was a pain. Such a pain, he thought he knew better than the man teaching us and ended up slicing his arm on his snowboard.

The splitboards were our transportation when we left the ski lodge. It was our way toward a new life. Most of the people in our group were fine. We weren't exactly friends with any of them then. We'd known the Dosens the longest and had made a commitment to help them get home, but we still didn't know them well.

It didn't take long to realize Jameson wasn't someone I wanted to be around. The first few weeks of our journey, I wanted to smack him daily. He was a snot. He talked terribly to the younger kids and even to his mom. I can't claim to be the perfect daughter, but I try and be respectful to my parents—and at least not mouth off to them in public.

Not Jameson, though. Some of the things I overheard him say were awful.

Somewhere along the way, he stopped being so annoying. I think maybe it was when we reached the small town of Roundup. We ended up staying there several days after Sadie and Sebastian Monroe, who used to be traveling with us but have settled at their aunt's place in Lewistown, were kidnapped.

While they were missing, Jameson was almost frantic. He kept saying how we had to find them, how he needed to apologize to Sadie for being such a brat. We did find them, and they were fine, with only minor injuries. Then Asher died, and everything was terrible.

Weeks later, when we were saying goodbye to the Monroes, I heard him ask Sadie to go on a walk with him. I think it was then he was able to make amends.

In the days following, the bratty Jameson became less and less, replaced with someone I almost liked. Then Nate died, and I stopped paying attention to him or anything else. Now, as I look at Jameson, I can see a new maturity, a growth that wasn't there before.

At fourteen, he's still a child, but we all have to grow up fast during the apocalypse. I'm seventeen, eighteen in November, and I have no doubt my life has fully changed. When we left the mountain, I wanted to make a difference, to be part of history as we rebuild our country.

I now wonder if that's even important. Do I want my name in history books, or do I want to be safe? I glance at my little sister. I definitely want her to be safe, my mom and dad too. Not only safe, but I want them to have the happy marriage they once did. They were like two beats of the same heart. Always in sync, always a team.

Now, I think they want to separate, each going their own direction. But how does separating or divorce work when the world has come to an end? When we're living essentially as nomads with no place to call our own?

The click of the radio pushes away my thoughts. "Bring your friends, Blondie. We're clear."

Blondie. My radio call sign. I hate it, but my dad thinks it's cute.

Patti, holding Trish in her arm with the radio on her hip, grins. "God is good . . . all the time."

Chapter 3

Kimba

I glance to the hilltop just in time to see my oldest daughter's blond head appear. "They're coming now. Rey called them over the radio."

"Okay, Kimba." Brett nods. "Do we wait for them here?"

I answer with a weary nod. "Stay sharp."

Nicole, too thin from months on the road, is pulling a rickety wagon loaded not only with our gear but also with her younger sister. Next to the girls is Patti Hyde, a woman who started traveling with us outside of Lewistown, Montana. She's pushing a stroller with her little boy in it and is wearing a fabric carrier across her chest to hold her infant daughter. Following them is Jameson, Victoria's youngest son, towing the body of our friend Jennifer on a homemade sled.

"Hi, Mommy." Naomi waves as they reach us. "I knew you'd be okay. The sun's almost ready to go down. Can we set up our tents now?"

"Soon, honey. We'll talk with Daddy first." I turn to Nicole. "Do you want me to handle the wagon?"

"I've got it." My daughter's tone is abrupt, and she doesn't meet my eyes.

Axel takes the handles of the sled from Jameson. "I'll take care of my mom."

Our pace to Rey and Atticus is quick. All of us are ready for this grueling day to end.

Two dozen feet away, Atticus's agitated voice carries across the ranch as he stands toe to toe with the big man, their height almost matching. "What do you mean, he might need some extra hands?"

The short woman sneers. "Just what I said."

Color rises to Atticus's cheeks. "This is our land, has been for over seventy-five years."

She points a bony finger at him. "Your folks owned the land, not you. And you just told us your mama died on the way here. Don't see your daddy. He dead too?"

Axel gently lowers the travois before moving next to his brother. "What's she saying, Atticus?"

"She thinks her dad owns our land. Squatter's rights."

Victoria lets out a huff. "That's not how squatter's rights work."

The woman smirks. "Oh yeah? Says who?"

"The law."

"There is no law." She cackles.

The big man, Scott, drops a beefy hand on the woman's shoulder. "Let's just— "

She shoots him a hateful look and pulls away.

He drops his shoulders and turns to Atticus. "Let's figure this out tomorrow. We'll talk to Lance. You all can stay in Miss Nina's house tonight. She isn't with you either?"

"We'll stay in our home." Axel steps forward.

"It's not your home!" the woman shouts. "You abandoned it. Can't you get that through your thick skulls?"

"C'mon, Tara." Scott's voice is low, pleading. "We'll sort it out tomorrow, after we bury Mrs. Dosen. She deserves a proper burial."

"Humph. She should've been a proper neighbor, then maybe things would be different. Do what you want, Scott. I'm going to bed." The woman spins on her heel and stomps away.

After the door slams, Scott turns to Atticus. "I'll help you with your mom. We'll sort it out. Lance—he'll probably be reasonable."

"This is our land." Atticus steps toward Scott. "*You* know that."

Scott nods. "Things are just . . . different now."

"You're with Tara?" Axel makes a face. "She's . . . not nice. Lance and Mouth—they aren't either."

"Tara's younger brother, Connor, is still here," Scott answers with a nod. "He'll be happy to see you."

Axel drops his chin. "We'll have to tell him about Asher."

"Atticus told me. I'm sorry. Your brother was a good guy, a good friend to Connor." Scott glances around our group. "Tara's okay once you get to know her. We're, um . . . we're getting married."

Atticus opens his mouth to say something, then seems to think better of it. With a shake of his head, he turns to Rey. "I'll show you to my aunt Nina's place. I'm going to put my mom in the root cellar— " His head spins back to Scott. "If that's all right with you?"

The man lifts his hands. "Yes, yes, of course."

Atticus turns toward Rey. "I'm staying with my mom until we bury her. Axel?" He lifts a hand in his brother's direction.

"Me too. I'll stay with her too."

"We'll figure this out tomorrow," Scott says again. "Lance'll be reasonable. I'm sure we can work this out."

Atticus turns back to Scott. "Lance will be leaving us alone. And you'll need to decide where your loyalty lies. The Double D belongs to us, to my brother and me."

"I know, I know." Scott lifts his hands. "It's just . . . you haven't been here. You don't know what we've gone through to keep things going. Lance stepped up, made sure I had the help I needed to get through the winter, through calving, all of it. It's only right he should have some compensation."

"Is that what you promised him? If he helped, he could have our ranch?"

Scott looks like he's been slapped. "I didn't make any promises. He just . . . it's not just your place. He took over the Laubin spread and a couple of others between here and Augusta."

"Figured he'd use the apocalypse as an excuse to get rich?" Rey asks.

Atticus scoffs. "He was already rich. He owned some big tech business, then sold it and thought he could be a rancher. At least he hired a decent foreman—someone who knew what he was doing, because Lance didn't know the difference between a bull and a cow."

"Miss Nina's place is locked." Scott fishes in his pocket, then pulls out a ring of keys and slowly peels two off. "It's pretty much how she left it. We don't spend time in there, so it might be a little out of sorts. And you'll need the key for the padlock on the root cellar too. I'll help you with your mom tomorrow, as soon as the sun's up."

"When did you move into our house?" Axel asks. "Your place not good enough for you?" He motions to a pair of cabins at the base of the hill.

"I, uh . . ." Scott shakes his head and lifts his hands.

"Let's just go." Atticus turns on his heel after giving Scott a long, angry look.

We follow the brothers to a smaller replica of the large ranch house. I lift Naomi out of the wagon. "You're getting almost too big for me to carry."

She bobs her head. "I'm too big for the wagon, too, Mommy. But as fast and as far as we walked, today it was good. Real beds tonight?"

"Let's get inside and we'll see."

The odor of the house assaults me first. It's stale and musty, having been locked up too long.

Axel wipes a hand across one of the tables. "Scott's right about it being out of sorts." He holds up a dusty finger. "But it hasn't been ransacked either. That's good at least."

"Let's open some windows." I move to the one nearest me.

"There are two bedrooms and an office," Atticus says, his voice weary. "The basement has a TV room with a sleeper sofa. Go ahead and make yourselves at home. I'm going to take care of Mom."

After the brothers shuffle back out the door, both looking many years older than they should, I turn to Rey. "Watch schedule for tonight?" My voice is clipped, much more than I intended. I'm too tired to care.

"I'll take watch," Brett and Jameson Dawson say in unison. The teenage brothers smile at each other.

Rey reaches for my hand; I hesitate before allowing him to take it. He gives me a quick squeeze. "We'll have two per shift, one inside and one outside. After last night and today, we're all pretty wiped. Victoria, are you up for a shift?"

I look to the older woman. Her jaw tightens, but her chaotic gray topknot bobs up and down as she agrees. Because of her aversion to firearms, we only have her on watch when we need a third person.

But last night, when the grizzly bear attacked, she fought the beast, first hitting it with one of her axes and then picking up Jennifer's revolver and popping off a couple of shots. Rey and the Dosen boys had sentry duty and quickly joined the encounter. As hard as they fought, it did little to stop the bear and the fatal damage inflicted on Jennifer.

At least they scared the bear away before anyone else was injured. Rey and some of the others went looking for it at dawn; we didn't want to be traipsing through the woods in the dark with a killer grizzly on the loose. They found a solid blood trail but no bear.

When we reached the nearby town of Simms, where we hoped to find medical care for Jennifer, we told them about the beast. They said they'd form a search party. Bears have been an issue in recent months, and this one needed to be dealt with.

With Victoria added to the watch schedule, Rey informs Patti she has the night off to stay with her young children and make sure they get the rest they need.

We take a quick tour of the house to sort out sleeping arrangements, not worrying about the grime and dust. After traveling by foot for almost five months, sleeping mostly on the ground, a little dust is nothing.

Patti and her children get the cozy basement. The Dawson boys take the second room with two twin beds. My girls are in the master with a queen bed. Victoria has the couch in the small office. Rey and I take the living room, me on the sofa and him in a recliner. I briefly consider saying I'll sleep in the room with our girls, but that'd be obvious. *Too obvious.*

As I tuck Naomi into bed, she gives me a sleepy smile. "I'm glad we're here."

"Me too, honey."

"Do you think the man will let us stay?"

"Don't worry about that tonight. You just rest."

"We'll bury Jennifer tomorrow?"

I give a slow nod.

Her eyes fill with tears. "I'm tired of people I love dying."

Chapter 4

Kimba
Friday, August 7

In the quiet of the early morning, I'm stationed on a berm to the east of the houses while Nicole is posted inside. We're on last watch—my preference. I take a deep breath, inhaling the earthy scents surrounding me. In the distance, a cow lets out a low bellow, and a horse brays in response.

Last night, after Brett and Victoria went to their watch stations and everyone else was in bed, Rey asked if we could discuss the situation with Atticus's neighbor. While we hope the man will be reasonable, we both doubt that'll happen. He'll repeat the things his daughter said about the Dosens abandoning the ranch and how there's no law.

What to do if the neighbor tries to lay claim to the land is where we disagree.

My opinion: walk away. The nearby town of Simms appeared to be doing well, working together and almost thriving, based on what I noticed when we traveled through. Axel and Atticus, along with Victoria and her boys, could make a life there.

Patti and her children are only staying through the winter before continuing to her family's Montana home on the Flathead Indian Reservation. They can stay in Simms as easily as on this ranch.

It really may be the better choice. While the Dosen brothers grew up ranching, the Dawsons didn't. They lived a rather cush life before our world fell apart.

Shoot, my life was pretty cush too. We had a successful consulting business, which provided us a spacious condo in Denver and an excellent living. We were comfortable and content.

Now that I look back on it, my life was definitely easy and full. But there was much missing. It wasn't fulfilling. Rey and I were so focused on business, we took little time to enjoy life. The children had all their activities and were running from place to place. Of course, then I had three children. And a happy marriage.

As the sun peeks over the horizon, my eyes fill with tears. My sweet Nate. His death is the most painful event I've ever experienced. Part of me died when we found his lifeless body. There's a smidgen of comfort in believing he didn't suffer. My hope is he was sound asleep and never woke up.

And I know he's in Heaven. One of the biggest changes in our family in recent months was asking Jesus to be Lord of our lives. Nate fully and completely gave his life to Christ, striving to live Biblically each day. The girls and Rey too.

And me . . . or so I thought.

Nate's death has diminished my passion. These days, I spend more time questioning God than praising Him. I imagine shaking my fist at Him—yelling and screaming, demanding answers. Why'd He take my son from me, from the world? Nate was a light, a beacon of hope and help.

I straighten my back as I glimpse movement near the main ranch house.

Tara, the woman living with Scott Pierce, slips around the edge of the building. Her stride is confident as she moves toward the barn. I track her movement until she steps behind a building.

Taking a deep breath, I ease back into position. As my mind wanders, I routinely scan the area, paying particular attention to where I last saw Tara. My diligence is rewarded about twenty minutes later when she reappears, this time on horseback.

She keeps the horse to a walk until she's past the house and other buildings, then brings it to a trot and takes the long driveway to the paved road. At the road, she turns west—the direction of her dad's ranch. A few moments later, she crests a hill and disappears from view.

As the sun illuminates the land, Atticus appears and makes a beeline for a small shed. When he steps out a few minutes later, he's awkwardly holding a couple of shovels and other garden tools.

The door to Nina's house, where we're staying, opens. Rey waves to Atticus. My watch time is over. It's now time to dig the grave, to say our final goodbye to another friend.

The first person we lost on this journey was Asher Dosen. His death was difficult. He died alongside two others in a small town we were stopped in. The funeral for the three was elaborate, a hero's funeral. The United States flag was raised, and we sang "The Star-Spangled Banner." At the end, a trumpeter played "Taps."

We buried Nate near where he died. No trumpet. No patriotic song. Just my small family and our few traveling friends. Atticus read from the Bible, we prayed, and Patti sang "Amazing Grace." At the end, part of my heart was buried with him.

Atticus chooses a beautiful spot slightly uphill from the ranch. Scott Pierce arrives with a post-hole digger. Patti and Victoria stay with Jennifer, preparing her for burial.

Scott says Tara emptied the Dosen closets, moving all their clothes to the basement and leaving them in a heap. Nicole and I find something from Nina's well-organized home for Jennifer to wear—a beautiful blue flowy skirt and button-up white blouse.

Axel returns often to the cool cellar to make sure someone is with his mom. I understand.

I could hardly bear to give up my son, even in death. When the digging is done and the body is moved graveside, I tell the brothers I'm going to help Patti bring the children over.

A few minutes later, we gather around. Bible in hand, Atticus clears his throat.

"Who's that?" Jameson points to someone on horseback entering the driveway. I squint slightly.

When I told Atticus and Rey about Tara leaving and how I thought she was probably going to her dad's ranch to tell him about us, they agreed. When Scott arrived to help with the digging, he confirmed this. But the rider isn't Tara.

"Connor Brower," Scott says. "He probably talked to Tara and came to give his respects to Mrs. D. He was fond of her."

A few weeks ago, Atticus was talking about their ranch. While there have been issues between the neighbors since Lance Brower bought the ranch a few years back, Connor became fast friends with all three boys, often riding horses together and just hanging out at the Dosens' house.

After a severe altercation between Connor's dad, Lance, and the Dosen boys' dad, Connor was forbidden from going to the Double D. Lance said he wasn't even supposed to talk to them in school. He disobeyed his dad and snuck over without any of the parents knowing.

Axel said Connor made a point of saying how much calmer life was on the Double D compared to his place. While Tara and Mouth, whose real name I have yet to learn, tolerate rural life, Connor loves it.

"Let's wait a minute," Axel says with a nod. "I'll go meet him and help with his horse."

When Axel returns with Connor, there're quick introductions. Although Connor's the same age as Atticus, he looks younger and rather effeminate with a tall forehead. I'm surprised when he shakes my hand with a firm grip and meets my eyes, his filled with tears.

After quick greetings all around, he turns to Atticus. "I'm glad you're here, back at the ranch. I can't believe Asher's dead. And your folks."

Atticus's mouth is a tight line. "Aunt Nina too. She died when . . . it doesn't matter. Let's get on with the service for my mom."

Once again, Patti sings—this time "How Great Thou Art"—and Atticus reads from the Bible. There's praying, of course, but my heart's not in it.

A few days ago, earlier in the evening before the bear attacked Jennifer, we had a mini church service. Atticus read a passage from Ephesians that really spoke to Rey. Like me, he's spent a lot of time blaming God for Nate's death.

Now Rey seems to be back in the fold, back to praying and reading the Bible, even wanting to read with me last night. I begged off, saying I was much too tired after the day we'd had.

It wasn't a lie. It just wasn't the entire truth. The truth is, I'm too angry.

God is God, right? I'm sure I read a passage somewhere in the Bible confirming God makes lightning and brings the wind. If He brings the winds, He must also bring tornadoes—tornadoes that come up out of nowhere and kill innocent little boys.

After Nate died, Jennifer said it's normal to blame God after a death, that it's part of the grieving process. She, too, experienced it with the death of Asher. She encouraged me to turn toward God instead of away from Him, and she'd often take my hands and pray with me.

Those first few days after Nate's death were the hardest. With Jennifer and Victoria also being injured in the storm, I felt so alone. Rey tried to comfort me, but he was hurting so much himself. We were a mess. And our girls, too, losing their brother . . .

I let out a deep breath.

And now Jennifer's dead. If God makes the lightning and brings the wind and has control of the entire earth, then that must mean even the grizzly bears. He could've prevented her death too.

As the service wraps up, I swipe at my watery eyes. Like Naomi, I'm tired of people we love dying. Rey wants to stay a few days, wait until Atticus and Axel have things sorted out with the neighbor.

I'm just done.

I've decided to stay at the ranch and end the walking. End many things, maybe even my marriage. My plan is to force Rey to leave, to continue on to Bozeman where our friends Chad and Beverly live—or at least they did before the world fell apart. Now, who knows?

He can go to them; the girls and I will stay here and start our lives fresh. Safe. That's all I want now. Safety. Security.

But we don't have either of those things here with the Dosens' crazy neighbor wanting their land. I've come up with a new plan: convince the others to move to Simms. Then I'll stay with Rey—for now—and continue on to Chad and Bev's.

We heard about buses running down I-15. By car, Great Falls to Butte, where I-15 meets I-90, is less than three hours. We even heard rumors there's another company offering rides on I-90. Capitalism has sprung up in the apocalypse. As the military and ordinary folks work to reestablish order, we'll see more and more of our old world return. Maybe someday we'll even find safety and security.

Our original plan was to check on Chad, Beverly, and their daughters, then settle in Billings for the winter. When we passed through the small city several months ago, the reconstruction efforts were in full swing. We all agreed it'd be a great place to make a difference. With the location close to our friends in Bakerville, we may even be able to visit them again.

Now I just want to hole up, do nothing until the spring, then go home to Denver.

When we fled our condo, minutes after Speer Bridge was destroyed in the coordinated terrorist attacks, we left with little, thinking we'd return within a few days. That was over a year ago.

I so wish I would've taken our photo albums. I *need* pictures of Nate. Rey has one of the five of us in his wallet. He gives it to me whenever I ask, but I need more. Nate's baby pictures, toddler pics, school—all of them.

I close my eyes. I wish I could hear his voice, could hold him one more time and tell him how much I love him.

"Mommy?" Naomi tugs on my arm. "Are you going to help cover Jennifer's grave?"

I blink several times before giving her a watery smile. "If they need me to. Then I think it'll be time for a snack. Are you getting hungry?"

"Did you hear Axel say he's going to hunt the bear that killed his mom?" Her eyes are wide and scared.

"He said that yesterday, but I'm not sure he still plans that today."

"He does! When you were helping Patti bring the babies out for the funeral, he said he's going into the little town, and if they haven't killed it, he'll kill it himself. He'll get . . . um, I can't remember the word."

"Vengeance?" I offer.

"Mm-hmm. Then Atticus told him to simmer down, but Axel said he's doing it anyway and his brother can't tell him what to do. Brett said he'd go into town with Axel and keep him out of trouble."

I shake my head. "I bet Axel appreciated that."

She lifts her tiny shoulders. "His face turned red. Then Atticus saw you and Patti and said we needed to start the funeral and they'd talk about it later."

"Uh, oh," Scott mutters, looking around. "Sounds like Lance is heading this way."

Chapter 5

Kimba

The hum of a car engine travels across the quiet land. "Great, just great." Axel stabs the tip of the shovel into the ground. "We don't even have Mom buried yet, and Lance is— "

"Maybe it'll be fine." Atticus rests a hand on his brother's shoulder.

Connor's face flushes. "Um, I need to . . . Dad doesn't know I'm here."

"Go on in the barn," Scott says. "We won't say anything." The big man glances at the rest of us, who nod or voice our agreement. The teen moves at double speed, taking a winding route to stay out of sight, as a small sports car pops over the ridge of the paved highway.

"I'll go meet them." Scott tilts his hat back slightly to wipe his forehead as he quickly walks away.

"Patti?" Rey motions with his arm. "Would you take Naomi and your children to the house? Victoria, join her?"

As Patti gathers up the babies, Victoria asks, "Will there be trouble?"

"I hope not. Keep watch, and have the rifle handy. Brett, you and Jameson grab your rifles and head to the outbuilding over there. Nicole, you take position beyond the berm. Everyone stay out of sight. Be ready. If it seems things are going bad, I'll take off my hat and say, 'It's going to be a hot one today.' That'll signal we're going pear-shaped."

"What about me?" Axel asks.

"I suspect the man will want to see you here. No doubt Tara's shared the details of your return, and our numbers, but no reason to flaunt it. It'll probably just be an easy conversation today."

"Humph," Atticus snorts.

"Kimba, dear?"

I raise my eyebrows in response.

"Let's have a bit of a show, love."

I stifle a sigh. "What'd you have in mind?"

"Oh, I think you know."

Nicole groans. "Please. Not that."

I roll my eyes. "It is a classic."

"It's annoying," my daughter says. "And insulting."

"To whom?"

"To you, Mom. The way you are so whiney . . ." Nicole shakes her head. "Besides, do you think someone like *that* would've made it this long? They'd be dead and— "

"Let's move, Nicole." Rey motions with his hands. "Everyone in position. Looks like someone's in the passenger's seat."

We all look toward the car as it slowly snakes its way down the main road. With the classic convertible—a late fifties or early sixties Ford Thunderbird in a lovely shade of baby blue—nearing the Double D driveway, I can just make out the two figures.

"Wonder where he got that," Atticus mutters.

My daughter makes a huffing sound. "Try not to embarrass me, Mom." She flounces off.

Brett and Jameson give each other a look and a shrug before heading to their spots.

"Keep working on the grave," Rey says. "Everything is normal. Kimba? Time's a wastin'."

I give a nod as I remove my utility belt. My sheathed knife goes in my pocket. The gun tucks into the small of my back, out of its holster. I hate carrying it there, but the long button-up shirt I'm wearing should camouflage it.

I wish I wouldn't have given Leanne Monroe the special tank top with an underarm holster and the little .380 that tucked in perfectly. I briefly consider asking Rey for his pocket pistol but decide, if I don't move around much, my gun will stay hidden. Plus, there's always the baby Glock with its single-stack, six-round magazine on my left ankle.

While some of our firepower was brought with Rey and me from Denver, most of it is thanks to our friends at the ski lodge. They were very good about outfitting us with the things we needed for this journey: camping gear, sturdy shoes, guns, and ammo.

Along the way, we've picked up a few other things as we scavenged empty houses. And meeting up with Patti increased our provisions, thanks to her and her husband's foresight and well-supplied caches buried in strategic locations.

Jennifer used to say it was God watching out for us, putting people and things in our path to help us along the way. *Miracles.* Now I'm beginning to think we were nothing but lucky, and our luck has run out.

I tuck the reworked utility belt into a bucket Scott brought out to help with the grave work. I remove the rubber band holding my hair at the nape of my neck, give it a quick shake, and let it rest on my shoulders.

I suck in my cheeks and purse my lips before giving them a smack. As I primly cross my ankles, ensuring the bulge of the holster is unnoticeable, I clear my throat and then nod at my husband.

"What are you doing?" Axel asks.

"Whatever she says or does," Rey responds, "just go with it."

"Like the shootout in Bridger?"

I lift my chin. "Exactly like that." Several months ago, at the checkpoint entering a small Montana town, a group of derelicts shot the guard and took Nicole and two others in our group hostage. My putting on a show took them off balance and gave us an advantage. That "show" was decidedly different than this one will be. And hopefully there will be no deaths or injuries involved this time.

As the car pulls alongside the ranch house, I plop myself on the ground. I agree with Nicole. This show will be annoying and insulting. But it could also serve a purpose. There was a time I loved to put on these acts. I found great satisfaction in pretending to be someone I wasn't. Now my heart isn't in it.

Rey and the Dosen brothers keep working on filling Jennifer's grave while Scott talks, motioning with his hands, as he walks toward us with Brower and his son.

I make a point of looking at the ground and picking at my fingernails.

When they're close, Atticus leans against his shovel. "Mr. Brower, Mouth." He gives the two a nod.

"Asher." Lance Brower returns the nod.

Axel makes a scoffing sound.

Atticus shoots his younger brother a look. "I'm Atticus, Mr. Brower. My twin, Asher, was killed a short time ago."

"Oh, yes. Tara told me about all your hardship. And this is your mom you're burying?" The man shakes his head and puts a pout on his face. "So sorry for your losses. First your daddy, then your brother, and now your mom. I suppose your aunt Nina was also killed somewhere along the way. Tara said she wasn't with you. Not easy for young men like you to handle."

"We're fine." Axel steps toward the older man.

After a glaring pause, Brower looks toward Rey. "Won't you introduce me to your friends?"

"Rey Hoffmann." Rey holds out his hand, introducing himself in his fake Midwestern accent with a slight whine in his voice. He lifts his chin in my direction. "My wife, Kim."

I glance at Brower and give a curt nod.

"Ma'am." He tips his hat and lowers his already deep voice. "I'm Lance Brower. This is my son Declan."

"Everyone calls me Mouth," the younger man says, his voice several decibels higher than I expect based on his likely age of early twenties and his robust size.

Axel snorts out a laugh, which earns him the evil eye from Mouth.

Lance ignores the interaction. "Tara said you have a couple of kids?"

I roll my eyes at the man before returning to my fingernails. My part to play is aloof and uninterested, complain and sniffle when given the opportunity.

It's the same show I put on during the early days of the collapse when we left Denver and found ourselves stranded in a campground outside of Shoshoni, Wyoming, where we met sisters Sylvia and Sabrina. I upped my whininess several degrees for them.

It was the best way to ensure they'd welcome us traveling with them, make them think Rey was a henpecked husband and our children in need of protection. From the moment we met them, it was obvious Sabrina was ready for the trek we had ahead of us. Sylvia not so much, but she was willing to follow her younger sister's lead.

The plan at the time was to stay with them as far as they were going: the small community of Bakerville on the Wyoming and Montana state line. I had no idea we'd find an old friend living there.

Well, she was a friend at one time anyway, before I made a colossal mistake that cost the life of her fiancé.

Rey clears his throat. "Please forgive my wife. The last few months have been . . . difficult."

"Understood." Lance answers. "I lost my wife several years ago. She, too, had . . . shall we say *issues* before her death."

I look up through my eyelashes to see the man turn to Atticus. "What are your plans, boy?"

"My plans? To finish burying our mom."

"Then I'm going into Simms," Axel says, "to make sure the grizzly that killed her is dead. If it's not, it will be before I return."

"I'm sure Scott told you there've been some changes in recent months." Lance lays a hand on his son's shoulder. "Declan and I, along with Tara, have been making a difference in this area. We're ensuring there's food for all until the government gets things up and running again."

"Oh, please." I screw up my face in disgust. "That's not what Tara said at all. She said your entire mission is to acquire as much land as possible before the officials come in and shut you down."

Mouth takes a step in my direction.

His dad moves a hand in front of his chest. "Well then, Mrs. Hoffmann— "

I raise my hand. "Not that I care. The things I've seen . . . stealing a little land is the least of it. I'm all in favor of getting ahead whenever possible."

Brower dips his chin at me. "I have the biggest spread around here. Both before the attacks and now. Pretty place."

"I'm sure it's lovely."

"It is. It truly is. After my wife died, we came here to start a new life. With the way things are now, we've stepped in to help those having trouble and offered to keep things going for them. And like with the Dosens here, when people were gone and left only their hired help holding the bag on everything, we've made sure they had what they needed. Isn't that right, Scott?"

Scott gives a barely noticeable nod before examining his dusty boots.

Atticus's jaw clenches as his hands tighten around the handle of the shovel.

"See there? I'm sure if these boys' folks were still alive, they'd be figuring out a way to thank my family properly. As it is . . ." He lifts his hands.

"What're you saying?" Atticus asks.

"Just letting you know we'll continue to help you out, to keep things going as they are. You and your friends can keep living in the small house— "

Axel takes another step toward Brower. "That's not— "

"Axel." Atticus shushes his brother. "Thanks for the offer, Mr. Brower. But now that we're home, we'll be fine on our own."

"Well, you see here . . ." Brower scratches at his clean-shaven chin. "It's not that simple. To make things more efficient, we've been running the cattle together, mingling the horses, breeding and all."

"I'm sure we can sort it out by brand."

Mouth crosses his arms and smirks. "We rebranded everything."

Atticus's face goes white and his jaw drops. "You rebranded our cattle?"

"Not your cattle, son. They were abandoned. When your folks didn't return in a timely manner, it became clear Scott couldn't handle everything on his own. Times have changed, boys. You two need to change with them."

Atticus takes a step forward. "Times *have* changed. The biggest change is we're home, back on the Double D. We'll be taking over the ranch for our folks, just like my parents always intended, just like my grandparents intended." Atticus tilts his head in Scott's direction. "You can stay and help us, or you can go on with Brower. Either way, we'll be moving back into our home, so you and Tara need to get your things out."

"Now you listen here, boy." Lance Brower steps into Atticus's space. "I don't think you understand how things are going to be— "

Atticus takes a step forward. "No, Mr. Brower. It's you who doesn't understand. We're home. This is our place. Your help is no longer needed nor wanted."

Brower lifts one side of his mouth. "That right? You know, you remind me of someone. What was his name, Declan? Oh, yes, Charley Laubin."

Scott visibly shudders.

Brower smiles. "I see Scott remembers Laubin. Scott probably also remembers the terrible incident at his place." Brower moves his head from side to side. "Just terrible. You see, one night, his house caught fire. Cattle stampeded. His poor family was attacked. All of them were shot and killed. It was a sad, sad thing."

Atticus narrows his eyes. "And I suppose you had nothing to do with it."

"Nothing at all. Fact is, had he accepted my help, the help from my crew, we could've kept him and his family safe."

Brower straightens, his voice becoming tight, icy. "You see, it's really best for all of us if we work together and keep things going as they are. As I already said, mine and your *folks'* cattle are mixed up. Now I'd be happy to find a place for you and your brother—even your friends here— "

I let out a cackle of a laugh. "Well, ain't that right kind of you. You're happy to steal these boys' ranch out from under them, but you'll give them a place to live? That's rich."

"Kim . . ." Rey's voice is low, warning. Slightly louder but with a pronounced whimper, he says, "We don't want trouble, sir. We just met up with these boys a spell back. Figured traveling together would be smart."

"What?" Axel gasps.

Atticus narrows his eyes. "Seemed smart at the time. Not so sure now."

"Say . . ." I smile up at Brower. "You wouldn't happen to have a cigarette, would you?"

The man smiles while his son lets out a hoot. "Cigarette? Those've been gone for a year at least."

I exaggerate a sigh. "Thought maybe since you all have been doing so well here, you'd have a stash."

Brower shakes his head. "Sorry. But if you're hankering for a steak and a stiff drink, I can help you out there."

He turns back to Atticus. "Look. I can see today's not the day to finalize our arrangements. You had a long walk—Tara told me all about your being stranded somewhere in Wyoming—and now you've lost your mom. I'm serious about the steak. Why don't you all come over tomorrow for some supper. We'll have ourselves a good talk, a party even. We'll feed your friends up well before they get on their way."

Atticus crosses his arms and lifts his chin.

"All right, then." Brower turns slightly toward Rey. "Nice meeting you folks. Tara said there were about a dozen of you. Where are the others?"

"In the house, resting."

"Make sure they all know they're welcome tomorrow. Scott, Tara's going to stay over at our place tonight. You come join her. It's not right for engaged people to be apart."

"Uh, okay. Later. I, uh, want to help with burying Mrs. D. Um, I'll walk you to your car."

After perfunctory goodbyes, the men walk away.

When they reach the Thunderbird, Axel turns to me. "What was that about? Why'd you act like that?"

I lift a shoulder.

"Why do you think?" Rey says.

Atticus dips the shovel in the dirt. "So he thinks we're weak. He's sure you and I are still just children. And now he thinks Rey and Kimba are . . . snivelers."

I snort out a laugh. "Snivelers?"

"But Scott . . ." Axel motions with his chin to the hired man starting back toward us. "Won't he tell them?"

"Tell them what?" Rey asks. "He doesn't know anything about us, does he? You didn't— "

"No, no." Axel shakes his head. "I haven't talked to him. But you weren't . . . you were normal before."

"We had little interaction with him," I say. "And now we keep up the ruse. I'm not so sure about the whole invite to dinner tomorrow night."

Rey shakes his head. "Yeah, my guess is Lance Brower has no intention of tomorrow night's dinner party."

"Then why ask us?" Axel asks.

Atticus throws another shovel of dirt on his mom's grave. "He told us his plans, didn't he?"

I nod.

"I think so," Rey agrees. "His story about Charley Laubin was a warning. Telling us Tara and Scott won't be here tonight, another warning."

Axel furrows his brow. "A warning for what?"

I let out another exaggerated sigh. "He plans to attack."

"Nope. He wouldn't." Axel shakes his head. "Why would Lance attack us? He can't be that . . . that . . ."

"Why not?" Atticus asks. "You know what he was like before, skirting the rules, the law. Now, as Tara reminded us, there is no law. He can do whatever he wants."

Axel pales. "We need to stop him. I'll . . . I'll see about getting help when I go into town. Maybe they have military there, or some sort of law enforcement."

"Let's finish here, then we can figure out what to do."

Chapter 6

Nicole

I press a finger against my temple. So much for thinking we could work things out. I guess, deep down, I knew there was going to be trouble.

Since Nate died, my mom has been saying we should've stayed at the ski lodge. We had it good there—plenty of food, a community, and safety . . . at least to a point. We had enough people we could fight back or fend off an attack. Now here we are, just a few of us trained to fight. And most, like me, aren't even trained well. Not well enough for a battle.

Mom and Dad are the exception, for sure. Both have a history of getting out of tight spots. They don't like to talk about it, and I didn't even know until last summer, but they used to be spies. Not spies exactly, and they hate that term, but what most people would think of as spies.

Dad worked for some branch of British intelligence, and Mom worked for the United States. Their paths had crossed a few times. Then something bad happened, something really bad. I don't know the details, but someone died, and Mom was blamed. She lost her job and was facing jailtime, or worse.

She ended up being officially cleared of any wrongdoing, but many still thought she was guilty. During that time, Mom and Dad became friends and eventually more. She was four months pregnant with me when they eloped.

Dad resigned from his government job, and they started our family. All my life I thought they had jobs as marketing consultants. Turns out, they were anything but marketing consultants. They were hired to fix problems. They insist they were still on the side of right, doing what they could to eliminate evil from the world. I'd like to think that's true.

If it is, this Lance Brower is definitely an evil that needs to be eliminated. The way he talks, sounding like he's just delivering a weather report, is wrong. How can anyone talk about an entire family dying without having even a hint of emotion in their voice?

I wish I could've seen his face. Would it have shown true sorrow? Or would it have been as fake as he sounded?

And an even bigger question, why'd my parents let him walk away? It's obvious he's a threat to us. Why let him leave? Why not just finish it here and now? Eliminate the threat? That's what they've been training us to do when we have our hand-to-hand combat lessons. Both say don't stop until the threat is gone.

"Nicole?" Mom calls to me.

I step out from my hiding spot in time to see Dad motioning the Dawson boys to join us.

"You heard?" Mom asks.

"Not all. I heard enough to know . . ." I lift my chin, motioning in the direction of the barn. "Here comes Scott and Connor. Should we— "

"Don't say anything," Dad warns.

The Dawson boys, Scott, and Connor Brower all reach us at about the same time.

Connor doesn't beat around the bush. "Scott says my dad made threats."

Keeping up the show, my mom whines, "Threats? I think that's a bit of an exaggeration."

Scott narrows his eyes. "It's not an exaggeration, ma'am. Lance aims to have this land. I thought— " He shakes his head before turning to Atticus. "Last night, when you all showed up, I thought we could maybe work something out, thought maybe Lance would be reasonable. I was wrong. He'll do whatever he thinks is necessary to keep running the Double D as his own."

Atticus throws his shovel aside and moves into Scott's space. Toe to toe with the older man, he speaks through clenched teeth. "Why'd you let this happen? We trusted you. My *dad* trusted you. When everything fell apart, he said we didn't need to worry, that you'd keep things going."

Scott drops his chin. "It wasn't that easy. You know how much work there is around here. You guys left before it got busy— purposely. It was the right time to go, get your sightseeing done, and get back. How'd you expect me to keep things going without electricity? And the work—I ain't never been afraid of hard work, but this is too much for one person."

Dropping his shoulders, Atticus nods. "Still, Lance Brower? Of everyone you could've gone to for help, why him?"

"You think I had a choice? He showed up here, him and Mouth, as nice as pie, telling me how we could let bygones be bygones. How as soon as you all got back, you'd be expecting to work together. No way any of us can survive any other way. It was fine, *at first.* Then things started to get strange. By the time winter hit and you were still gone . . . well, I figured you just weren't coming back. What would you think?"

"You just let him have our place?" Axel sneers.

"It wasn't like that. At first, it was just a little help. He'd send his men over. He had, what? Four, five guys working for him, plus his foreman EJ Martin and the household staff? Now he's got a couple dozen, added some women too. At least one of them . . ." He shakes his head as his voice trails off.

Mom's and Dad's eyes meet. The unspoken communication is obvious. Things are bad. Really bad.

"Connor?" My mom's voice is light, carefree. "Surely you don't really believe your dad . . ." She gives a brilliant smile while lifting her shoulders.

Connor answers with a slow shake of his head. "My dad is not a good guy. He's always been out for himself, willing to do whatever's needed to get ahead. It got worse after my mom died. It was like his little bit of humanity, of morality, left with her. Now . . ." He lifts a hand.

"Mouth's no better. And Tara— " Connor looks to Scott. "She just does what she wants. Dad's always called her his princess, and that's how she still lives. She doesn't lift a finger toward the day-to-day survival, does she, Scott?"

Scott's face turns crimson. "She's, um, delicate."

Connor scoffs. "Lazy. She's lazy."

"Now see here, Connor. That's my fiancée you're talking about."

"And my sister. But really, Scott, you can't truly believe you'll get married. You asked her, when? Over the winter? She's been putting you off since then, right?"

"We're waiting until things get more normal so we can have a proper wedding, a honeymoon even."

Connor waves a hand. "Whatever. I'm just saying, my sister does what she does to make her life easier. If Dad's cooks and housekeepers didn't come over here, you wouldn't even have any food or clean clothes. Tara's not doing it. How does she spend her days? Reading or riding her horse, right?"

Connor turns toward Rey. "You folks would be smart to pack up and move on. Get back into Simms, they'll let you settle there. Atticus, you and Axel too."

"We're not leaving." Axel's voice is firm.

"He'll kill you, just like he did Charley Laubin and his family. Well, *he* won't do it, not himself. But he'll get his men to do it. He'll stay at the house, holed up in his study, reading his books and waiting for the report. Just like Tara, he doesn't do much. He just orders others around."

"Why do you stay here?" I ask, my words rushing out. "I mean, it doesn't sound as if you like your dad or sister too much, so why stay?"

"Where would I go? I'm . . . look at me?" He motions to his body.

"So?" I put a hand on my hip. "We've met a lot of people. Size doesn't mean much. It's what you've got in here." I move a finger to my temple before sliding it down to my chest. "And here."

"Leave him alone, Nicole," my mom whines. "He's smart to stay here where things are easy."

I roll my eyes at her. She may be faking, but it's still annoying. "Sure, Mom. You're just jealous you don't have the easy life. Maybe you'd like to go to that big farmhouse and tell this guy's dad how we should stay here."

"Maybe I will." She raises her eyebrows. "In fact, Rey, *honey*, that's a good idea. Let's make a deal—a deal for all of us to stay and work with him. Last night, Scott said he'd need more hired men."

"No. No way." Axel shakes his head. "You're nuts if— "

Atticus puts a hand on his brother's arm. With a slight shake of his head, he says, "Knock it off. Don't talk to Kimba—*Kim*—like that. She's . . . you know how it's been for her. You know, since the show."

Axel narrows his eyes. "Since the show . . . okay."

"You think he'd talk to us?" Mom bats her eyelashes at Connor.

Ick. I feel a little sick to my stomach over the manipulation. I think Connor is just what he says he is: not a part of his dad's plans to take over all the land. But I know we can't risk it.

Scott may have given us a warning that Brower plans to attack tonight, but Brower probably told him to do it and encourage us to leave. I doubt Brower cares one way or another. People like him . . . he may have skirted the law before, but now he has nothing to lose. He might as well kill to get what he wants.

Connor lifts a shoulder. "Not sure. I supposed he'd at least talk to you."

Mom makes a pouty face. "Can we go, Rey? See if we can make a deal? I'm tired of traveling. I'd like to winter here, rest up."

"How is it you think this could work?" Scott asks, looking from my mom to my dad before glancing at the Dosen brothers. "Brower may let you stay, but he won't give the boys their place back. Not by choice."

Mom flips her hair. "Maybe the boys can just accept this is for the best?"

"Humph." Axel spins on his heel and stomps away.

Jameson and Brett shake their heads in unison and follow Axel. From the looks on their faces, they think my mom has lost it, that Kimba Hoffmann is succumbing to the grief of losing her only son. She's calling it quits and falling in with the enemy. They may be right.

"Way to go, Mom," I mutter as I follow the boys. She's faking it, at least I hope she is, but it's still a terrible thing to see. My mom wimping out . . . I hate it.

Chapter 7

Kimba

I let out a quiet breath through my nose. Nicole, Axel, and the Dawson boys stomping away is good; it'll help with the ruse.

I straighten my spine and put on my finest, fakest smile. "Atticus, surely you can see how this is best. We traveled so far. You've lost so much. Why risk losing more? You and your brother could be killed."

"*Would* be killed, Mrs. Hoffmann." Scott nods. "No doubt about that. They'd make sure of it."

"Whose side are you on here?" Atticus asks Scott.

"The side of no more dying. There's been enough." He motions to the grave. "Let's finish burying your mama, then you can decide what you're doing. Like Connor said, you could go back to Simms. You have friends there. They'd let you stay."

Scott turns slightly toward me. "I don't think making a deal with Mr. Brower is a good idea. You seem like nice enough folks. But with the young 'uns, I'd think you'd be better off moving on."

"Meaning?" Rey asks.

"Scott's probably right," Connor says. "There're no children here. Not with any of the hired help—not even the household help."

"And not on any of the ranches Mr. Brower added to his spread," Scott says. "Charley Laubin had children, but they, uh . . . the entire family died in the fire."

"*Fire.*" Connor shakes his head. "The fire came after the shooting."

Throwing another shovel of dirt, Atticus keeps his eyes on the slowly closing grave. "I'm not going to just let him take our land. My dad wouldn't stand for Brower doing this, and neither will I."

"Your dad was smart," Scott says. "And he knew when he was licked. You'd be smart to realize it too."

"My dad never quit."

"That's true. But he did know enough not to beat his head against a wall to try and move it. If your dad were here, he'd bide his time. Someday, law and order's bound to return. You can sort things out then, get the courts involved. You can't do that if you're dead."

I heft myself off the ground. "See? Scott thinks it's smart. Connor?"

"Like I said, you can try. You shouldn't trust him, though. He'll look you in the eye, shake your hand, and still stab you in the back the first chance he gets." The young man raises a hand to his sparsely whiskered jaw. I notice a bruise, faded to yellow.

The men mutter and talk while they finish the grave, and I realize it might take some doing to get my utility belt out of the bucket without looking suspicious.

My problem is solved when Scott turns to me. "Thought I'd start hauling some of the tools back to the shed. Figured you'll be wanting to empty out the pail 'fore I take it away."

I lift my chin and give him a smile. "As far as I'm concerned, you could take that silly thing with you. I only wear it to make my husband happy. He's into the whole Boy Scout thing, you know."

"That right? Seems 'Be prepared' is a smart motto to follow these days. Probably was before too. My daddy taught me to never leave the house without a knife in my pocket. But I'm surprised your husband was a Boy Scout."

"Why's that?"

"Isn't he a foreigner?"

My heart rate speeds up as I force a laugh. "*Foreigner?*"

"Well . . . thought I heard an accent when he was talking with the boys earlier. Slight, but there. But I don't hear it when he talks to me or when Brower was here."

Overhearing the conversation, Rey steps near us. "You're right, Scott," he says in his Midwest voice. "I had a speech problem as a child. Not a lisp, but something like it. Kids teased me something awful. I've worked hard to rid myself of it, but it still slips out sometimes."

A look of understanding and then embarrassment crosses Scott's face. "Ah, well, um, I see. Sorry 'bout that. I didn't know." He lifts his hands.

"No problem. How could you know? And in answer to your other question, I was never a Boy Scout. But it does seem prudent to be ready for anything in today's world. Now if I could only get my wife on board."

I flip my hand in the air. "We won't need all that stuff if we can find someplace safe to stay. Once we work things out with Brower,

I'll be happy to say goodbye to the awful, heavy belt for good and find a nice flowy dress to enjoy the last days of summer."

Axel and the Dawson boys reappear to help with the grave. Nicole gives me a determined look as she stalks off toward the house.

After the grave is filled, everyone stands around as the boys say their final goodbyes.

"Connor?" Scott lifts a hand toward the younger man. "Wanna join me in the house? I suspect these folks have some decisions to make and don't need us hanging around."

"I'd best go on home. Um . . ." Connor turns to Atticus. "Look, I just want to say, I know what my dad's doing sucks. It's wrong, and you should fight it—fight him. But he's got too many men now. And some of them . . . well, killing doesn't bother them, not now when there aren't any consequences. Maybe it never did. Scott's probably right. You bide your time, wait it out in Simms, and things are bound to improve later."

Atticus gives a barely perceptible dip of his chin.

"Nope." Axel shakes his head. "Not happening. But I was thinking I'd take a ride into town to find us some help."

"Best not," Scott says. "There're folks loyal to him there. Not many, but enough you can't trust it wouldn't get back to him. And there was some truth to what he said. He has been keeping the town fed and sharing the cattle."

"And booze," Connor adds. "My dad's been getting grain from wherever he can find it to make hard liquor. He makes wine out of fruit and flowers too. Says he may even be making beer soon."

"Yup." Scott nods. "He has plenty of fans, thanks to the alcohol."

Axel straightens. "I'm not giving up."

Connor nods. "I understand. Just think about it. You didn't come all this way to end up dead."

"You could help us stop him."

"Not without killing him. I— " He shakes his head. "I can't do that." Again, his hand goes to his bruised jaw.

Scott and Connor head toward the big house while the rest of us go to the smaller one. Once inside, we catch Patti and Victoria up on what we think we know from Brower's visit.

"We were watching from the window," Patti says.

"Mm-hmm." Victoria smiles. "Saw you flipping your hair a lot."

"Moi?" I put my hands to my chest, acting shocked. "Why, I'd never use my feminine wiles on a man to try and get him to lower his guard."

"That's not all she did," Axel says. "She pretended to be weak, a coward. I didn't like it. And I definitely don't understand it. Why act like some brainless woman instead of who you are?"

"Because— "

"I know. You said so Brower would think we weren't a threat. But really, how does it help? You all just want to give our place to him anyway, so what does it matter?"

I suck on my top lip while motioning with my eyes to Rey.

"This really isn't our decision," my husband says. "It's up to you and your brother. I'll admit, since we arrived, I've been of the mind this is your place and you should make your stand."

"That's right." Axel nods.

Rey raises a hand. "But after meeting Brower and hearing how he was so matter of fact about things without remorse, things are different now. Scott may think you can work something out with him, be Brower's slave or something like it and you'll be able to live here. I don't think he'll let that happen." Rey shakes his head.

"Let Kimba and I go over there. We'll go under the pretense of making a deal with him, an arrangement to stay. Hopefully, we'll get info about his men. Connor and Scott gave us some good clues, but we can't know if they're being entirely truthful."

Atticus clicks his tongue. "Connor hates his dad."

"Maybe he does. But there's still a bond there, and those bonds— " Rey lifts his hands. "Plus, Scott's marrying Brower's daughter."

"Why, I'll never understand." Atticus scrunches up his face. "She may be pretty, but she's as bad as her dad. In fact, the way Kimba was acting was really a toned-down version of Tara. She's always been a whiner."

"And the oldest boy, Declan? He's always been by his dad's side?"

"More like in his shadow. Usually, Mouth can't do anything right, and his dad lets him know."

"Been there," Jameson mutters under his breath.

Jameson and Brett have been through some things. Their dad abused them for years. Then, after the attacks and EMP, he saw a way to exert his power and influence. What may have started as good intentions, as a way to help his community, turned into something awful when things didn't go exactly the way he wanted. He ended up dead from his efforts.

Jameson and Brett's dad isn't the only one we know of who's used the apocalypse to their advantage. A man in Prospect, Wyoming—Richard Majors—along with his son, took over the town and killed anyone who provided opposition. Not satisfied with having just a town under his thumb, he's branched out to control the region.

A month before we left the ski lodge, he attacked and killed those from our small community who didn't move up the mountain with us.

Leaving the lodge, knowing a madman was still on the loose, was hard for us. If we wouldn't have committed to getting Jennifer and her sons home, we would've stayed and made sure Richard Majors was stopped.

Now here we are. We got the Dosen boys home, but what good did it do? And I don't know if I have any fight left in me to stop Lance Brower. Losing Nate . . . I let out a breath through my nose, pushing thoughts of my son aside.

"From the sounds of it, Brower doesn't get his hands dirty," Rey says. "He lets his men do the killing. Mouth probably stays with his dad. To end this, we'd need to kill both father and son. Maybe Tara too."

Atticus and Axel both go pale.

"We can't— " Axel shakes his head. "Can't we just make a deal?"

"Not without looking over your shoulder every day."

"You don't know that. Lance used to be a businessman. He'd honor a deal."

"You're willing to stake your life on it? Even his son said he'd stab you in the back."

Letting out a long, noisy breath, Atticus turns to his brother. "Rey's right. Our choices are to be willing to kill them all or scurry away with our tails between our legs."

Rey clenches his jaw. "That's about the size of it."

"What about Connor?" Axel asks. "We wouldn't— "

"Connor's probably just what he seems." Rey lifts a hand. "But if we kill his dad and brother, things could change."

"We'd need to secure him," I say. "Scott too. Then, when it's all done, we evaluate."

There are several moments of silence before Atticus says, "You're sure about going to his place? You don't think . . . Lance wouldn't just kill you then?"

"There's always that chance," Rey answers. "But I don't think he looks at us as a threat. Kimba's antics amused him. She'll play it up a little more when we're there. And I'll play the simpering fool, unhappy in my marriage and looking for something different."

"I'm not sure that's the right play." I tilt my head. "From what Connor said, his dad has surrounded himself with killers. It might be best to let him know you'd be willing to play the part so you can get more info out of him."

Rey scrunches his nose. "Perhaps. We'll adjust as needed."

"And what do we do while you're at Brower's?" Axel asks.

"We'll need some early warning systems put in place, should we decide to stay and fight. I'm hopeful our visit today will, at the very least, buy us some time and convince him we're not worth attacking. But if not, we need to be ready. Atticus, you had a hand in the noisemakers we constructed at the ski lodge, the ones near the observation posts?"

"We both did." He motions to his brother. "Our dad used to reload his ammunition. He had a bunch of primers."

"Yeah." Axel makes a face. "If they weren't stolen. There're mouse traps in the cellar—we saw them last night. We can make those mouse trap alarms like we used near the listening posts."

"Sounds like a plan," Rey says.

"He had a nail gun too." Atticus flicks his eyebrows. "That could make a good alarm."

"See what you can come up with."

"I'd still like to go into town and find out about the bear," Axel insists.

"Depending on how things go with Brower, we might all be going into town," I say.

"I'm not running away."

I dip my head in concession. One thing's for sure, Axel is determined. Both he and Atticus have fight in them. Brett, Jameson, and Nicole too. All of them will do what's needed.

But they could end up dead.

I'm not willing to let that happen. If keeping these teens and my daughters alive means we, as Atticus said, scurry away with our tails between our legs, then we do it. We can set up the Dosen brothers, the Dawsons, and Patti and her children in Simms. They'll be fine there.

Then Rey, the girls, and I can get back on track to Bozeman. Maybe there I can get my head on straight, get out from under this terrible grief. Maybe I'll even want to be with my husband again. Then, eventually, we can go home to Denver.

I hate that part of me hopes, when we get to Brower's ranch, we'll discover he has a hundred hired killers and there's nothing we can do. Of course, if they moved to Simms, could we trust that Axel wouldn't go off half-baked? Knowing the boy, he just might try and drum up his own little army to eliminate Brower—and get himself killed in the process.

Great. Another no-win situation. I wish I'd stop getting myself in the middle of these.

Chapter 8

Kimba

Atticus suggests we take horses to Brower's ranch. While Rey and I have ridden before, neither of us are overly comfortable on horseback. So we're on foot, walking at a fast clip to cover some ground. Once the ranch comes into view, we'll stroll in, all leisurely like.

While we're gone, Atticus and the rest will set up a variety of booby traps and noisemakers to give us a heads up if anyone approaches, even in the dark. Patti said she has a few ideas, too, things her husband helped set up around the Mosher compound in Lewistown.

Rey reaches for my hand. "There it is."

I stiffen before letting my hand relax in his. When did his touch start feeling so foreign?

"Wow. His place is huge." We slow to a walk.

When planning this, we agreed to go in looking unprepared, each of us just carrying small packs. Brower already saw Rey with a gun on his hip, so he left it in place. We fully expect to be required to surrender the sidearm before seeing Brower. And we expect our bags to be searched.

Once again, I wish for the underarm holster and pistol. Instead, I'm carrying a .22 Taurus belonging to Nicole. It's not my favorite, but when it's low on my hips in a bellyband holster, it leaves less of an imprint than the full-sized 9-millimeter Glock 17.

The .22 isn't great for self-defense, but we know if I must use it, it'll be up close and personal. The small caliber bullet can do some serious damage, rolling around internally. Plus, it's a nine-shot wheelgun that's unlikely to malfunction. While the seventeen-round magazine, plus one in the chamber, of the Glock is superior firepower, I could do worse.

Rey's wearing cargo pants with his holstered small pistol tucked deep in the left-hand pocket. As the holder of a concealed carry permit, he's had the gun for years, even before the world fell apart. He'd often take it with him on business trips, secured in his checked luggage. Of course, when he needed something larger than a .380

tucked in his pants pocket for his "consulting" jobs, it was the responsibility of the employer to provide on location.

When we left Denver on the day of the bridge explosion, we'd each brought a couple of personal weapons, keeping them well out of view. And when we met Sabrina and Sylvia, I played my part so well they were convinced I was not only anti-gun but also a disarmament advocate.

I smile at the memory of just how annoying I was. I'm sure Sylvia wanted to pop me more than once. But she never suspected I was carrying not one, but two sidearms. Of course, she never patted me down either.

I certainly hope whoever checks us for weapons is on the squeamish side and not comfortable putting hands on me. Rey and I each have a knife on us, too, which we hope will go unnoticed. There's certainly the chance they'll kill us. Or try to. I'm not going down without a fight.

We've given our group strict orders to hightail it to Simms if we aren't back by sundown. I doubt the Dosen boys will obey, but I'm confident Victoria will ensure our children, Patti's family, and her boys are safe.

Rey lets out a low whistle. "It's not just huge, it's extravagant. Looks like it was plucked right off the Italian countryside. Check it out, he's got solar too. I wonder if it's working?"

"Well la-di-da. No wonder he looked at Atticus and Axel like they were dirt poor farmers. Their place is nice, gorgeous even. But this . . ."

"It's something, for sure. Must be close to ten thousand square feet. They've noticed us." Rey lifts his chin toward the house as we turn on to a two-track gravel drive. I quell a smile as we watch people scurry around.

"Keeping up the act just between us?" I squeeze my husband's hand.

"Whatcha mean?"

"I've noticed you've used your fake persona since we met Brower earlier."

"After what Scott said, I didn't want to risk it. Besides, it's easier than switching back and forth."

"This—all of this—I'm about done with it."

"I know, Kimba. We made a mistake, didn't we?"

I bite my top lip, willing the tears away. "We should've stayed." My voice cracks. "Or at least left the children with Doris, taken her up on her offer."

We take a dozen steps in silence.

"I miss him so much." Rey's voice is low, gravely.

I clear my throat. "Here they come."

Three men climb into an old pickup truck—two in the front and one in the bed, his rifle at the ready. They creep their way toward us, stopping fifty feet away.

A rugged, overly tan man steps from the passenger's side. "Howdy, folks. Something we can help you with?"

"Hey, there. My wife and I, we met Mr. Brower earlier. He said we should stop by sometime, so . . ." Rey lifts a hand.

"That right?"

"We're staying at the Dosen place."

The man gives a slow nod. "Heard the boys made it back. Too bad about their folks. They were good people."

"I'm sure they'd appreciate you paying your respects," I say.

"Yeah, well . . ."

"Are you Martin?" I ask. "The foreman?"

"Yup. EJ Martin."

We're close enough now I can make out the deep wrinkles around his eyes and mouth. "We'll drive you the rest of the way. I'll make sure Mr. Brower is willing to visit."

"That's very kind of you." I smile and bat my eyes.

EJ Martin motions to the man in the bed of the truck. "How about you help our guests here." He turns back to us. "Afraid I'm going to need to take that peacemaker off you." He motions to Rey's hip.

Before we left the house, he swapped out his Glock for a Ruger .45 Colt double-action stainless revolver from one of the caches Patti and her husband set up. The well-oiled gun had been wrapped and protected, straight out of the factory. And the box of ammo was a welcome addition to our supplies.

Martin also gives a cursory glance inside my messenger bag and Rey's daypack. Neither of us are patted down—good for us, but not smart on their part.

"Climb on in." He motions to the truck.

As we near the house, it's even lovelier up close. The truck pulls around a large, tree-lined, circular driveway and parks next to the blue Thunderbird.

I'm impressed to see how well the estate has been cared for. Everything is neatly trimmed and weeded. Even the pavement looks freshly swept. The only sign we're in the middle of the apocalypse is the nonworking fountain in the middle of the driveway. Its classic three-level Italian design, with a smooth finial on top, is the perfect centerpiece.

Martin tells us to get out of the truck and wait a moment as he goes to the house.

The driver of the pickup and the man in the bed walk away. A quick glance around tells me *they* may be uninterested, but there're others around who are paying plenty close attention to us.

One guy, wearing a red ballcap, is holding a carbine in low-ready position. When his eyes meet mine, a chill runs down my back. I've met men like him, women too—soulless people who have no trouble with killing.

Martin walks toward us with a slight limp on his right. He gives me a kind smile. "Head on up to the door. They're expecting you." He motions to the palatial house.

Leaving the front door wide open, Mouth meets us on the covered stone porch. "Thought Dad said to come for supper *tomorrow?*"

"Oh?" I flutter my eyes. "Did I misunderstand? I thought we were given an open invitation to see his ranch? Maybe even get a tour?"

Mouth furrows his brow. "He did? I don't— "

"Just bring 'em on in, Declan." Lance's deep boom carries from somewhere inside.

The younger man shakes his head. Once inside, he motions for us to follow him.

From the foyer, we get a glimpse of the formal, and very white, austere living room. The marble covering the floor of the entry continues as far as the eye can see. Declan, or Mouth, I have no idea what to call him, takes us to the left of the front door.

"Well, Mr. and Mrs. Hoffmann, I'm s'prised to see you." Lance Brower stands near a double door and sways slightly as he greets us, a near empty tumbler in his hand, the alcohol on his breath noticeable.

Rey reaches out a hand. "Rey. Please call me Rey."

"A'right. Rey it is."

I give him what I hope is an award-winning smile. "Your son indicated we may have misunderstood your invitation. When you said how lovely your home is—and oh my, it certainly is—I thought you were suggesting we visit. Please forgive the intrusion."

"No, no. No intrusion. You are, of course, most welcome. Always happy to show off my home and the ranch. Want the tour?"

"Oh, yes, please."

He reaches inside the room and loudly plops his glass on a table. "Well, let's go then."

He escorts us through the house, pointing out the various features and appointments. From the second floor, I marvel at the open balconies overlooking the main level.

"Daddy?" Tara steps out of a room near the front of the house, over the area we first met Lance Brower.

"Darling," Lance beams at his daughter. "You remember the Hoffmanns?"

She huffs out a breath. "What are *they* doing here?"

"Visiting, being neighborly."

"Really?" She shakes her head and returns to her room, slamming the door.

Brower smiles indulgently at the closed door. "Ah, well. Tara . . . growing up during her formative teenage years without a mother wasn't easy. And now, with the troubles . . ." His voice fades away before he perks up and says, "Did I show you the elevator? It doesn't work now, of course. But what a help it was."

We go back to the main stairs. "There it is. Martin said he might be able to rewire it and then tie it into the solar system. We'll see."

I motion to a half flight of stairs. "Does this go to the master?"

"Oh, goodness no. I'd never want a second-floor master. Terrible for resale. This is Declan's room. Each of the kids' rooms and the guest room has a private bath—that's a help for resale." His face crumples slightly.

"Not that that matters much now. Anyway, Declan is here. Tara spends most of her time at the ranch with Scott, but is here on occasion—slamming doors." He gives a wry smile as he motions to her bedroom. Even knowing who this man is—what he does—I can see how he's been so successful in life with his amicable ways.

"Down the hall from Tara is my youngest son's room." He motions with his arm. "He doesn't spend much time outside of the bedroom unless he's off riding his horse. Prefers his books to our company."

Neither Rey nor I say anything about already having met Connor. And neither of us mention the disdain we hear in Brower's voice when speaking of his youngest. My thoughts return to the bruise along Connor's jaw and my suspicion his dad is the cause of the mark.

My stomach tightens. Friendly or not, anyone who would do that to his own child . . .

"Let's go this way." Lance motions to the back of the house. "I'll show you the guest room, then we'll be finished on this level."

Rey points to a large chandelier. "We noticed your solar array. Did it survive the EMP?"

"Mostly. Had to do a little rewiring, but we got it going again. Lost a couple of batteries somehow. They just burned up. One of my men was able to disconnect things we don't absolutely need, like my beautiful light." He shakes his head and lets out a sigh.

"But we have light in the bedrooms, a small fridge, and even a chest freezer in the basement. What would life be without rocks for my Scotch? We're doing fine."

I paste a smile on my face. *Yeah.* Life would certainly be rough if he couldn't have his ice cubes.

We soon find ourselves in the family room off the large kitchen. The home truly is beautiful. Even the changes made post-EMP are upscale. Brower ushers us to the wall of glass at the back of the house.

"Oh my," I exalt in a breathy voice. "This is amazing."

Brower grins pridefully. "It's an accordion-style door. Ever see one?"

"How does it work?" I ask, feigning ignorance. I've not only seen these doors before, but both our residence condo and office condo in Denver had them. They were the perfect way to expand the rooms and bring our small balconies into our living spaces.

As Brower demonstrates opening each side, folding the windows into themselves, causing the door opening to span the entire length of the wall, Rey's eyes move to the lever knob.

"Pretty amazing." Rey nods. "Mind if I try closing it?"

"Have at it." Brower steps back, giving Rey directions for the simple task. I notice Rey runs a finger along the locking mechanism where the two sides of the bi-fold door connect.

"There isn't even a fingerprint or smudge on the glass. You must have quite a staff." I motion to the severe woman in the kitchen.

"Oh, a few." Brower waves a hand. "Twila was my cook before we even moved here. She came with us from California. So did Becca, she takes care of the housekeeping. We have . . ." He looks to the cook and raises his voice. "What, six more?"

"Eight. My two helpers here in the kitchen— " She motions to a couple of girls around Nicole's age. "Becca has three, and we have Sidney and the other two working outside in the garden and such. With the extra work involved, everything takes longer."

"And it's all so much work," I say. "I mean, just making a meal is an all-day event. And don't even get me started on laundry."

She narrows her eyes, apparently less than impressed with my lamenting. "Indeed."

"What about your hired men?" Rey motions with his hand. "Do they join you for dinner in your fancy dining room?"

Lance looks shocked. "Um, no. Twila and her staff make the food. A few of the men come and pick it up."

"At the backdoor." Twila motions to a door off the kitchen.

"Oh, of course." Rey nods. "So, it's just the family and household staff at meals. That makes sense."

Twila rolls her eyes. "The household staff, as you put it, enjoy our own dining room in the basement."

"Like *Downton Abbey*?" I ask.

She gives me a hard look. "Do I look English to you?"

It takes all my composure not to burst out laughing. I don't even dare look at my British husband, sporting his fake accent.

"Ah, but the difference is," Brower says, lifting his chin toward the housekeeper, "Twila doesn't sleep in the attic like a little mouse. She has her own lovely apartment downstairs. Becca also—from before. The others, we've done a little rearranging so they can all be comfortable. Much better than some of the other options, right, Twila?"

"Yes, sir." The severe woman nods. "We're all very grateful to have so many comforts during such a time."

Brower puffs up his chest and gives a Cheshire grin. "It's the least I can do for those less fortunate."

Twila dips her head again and returns to her work.

"Shall we go back to the study?" Lance asks.

"Do we not get to see your bedroom?" I bat my eyes again.

After padding across a marble-tiled hallway, separating the formal dining room and living room, he throws open a set of massive double doors. He shows us an extravagant bathroom before leading us down a short hallway to a huge master. Everything is perfect and neat as a pin.

"It's lovely," I gush.

He cocks an eyebrow and licks his lips. "Indeed."

"Uh, yeah." Rey reaches for my hand. "Nice place. Good thing you have so many fireplaces." He motions to the open hearth between two glass doors, also accordion style but with only a single fold on each side instead of the multi-fold of the family room doors.

"It was still cold as the dickens last winter. Could hardly stay warm. But with a wood burner in each bedroom, my study, the living room, and family room, it was bearable. Martin said we should try and find inserts before this winter so we use less wood, but I just can't bear the idea of changing things so much. It's bad enough what we had to do in the kitchen, moving out the commercial range and replacing it with a woodburning stove. That was almost sacrilege. Shall we move back to the study?"

Once in the smaller room, he makes his way to a bar cart. "Can I make you a drink?"

"You truly have Scotch?" Rey asks, pretending surprise.

"I have a still." He gives us a wink as he pours himself a shot and quickly downs it. The face he makes tells me it's not the caliber of booze from before the lights went out.

We both pass on the drinks but accept the chairs he offers—not the cozy chairs in the sitting area with a couch and coffee table, but two uncomfortable looking chairs by the desk.

Lance Brower makes a second, triple-shot drink, this time adding a couple of ice cubes from a bucket, before slipping behind his massive desk. He leans back in his chair and laces his hands behind his head. "You enjoyed the tour?"

"Very much," I rave. "It's such a lovely home."

Rey dips his chin. "I've never seen anything quite like it."

Lance lifts his lips in something resembling a smile. "I'm sure. Now, should we get down to why you're really here?"

"Why, Mr. Brower, whatever do you mean?" I ask, giving him my best smile.

Rey reaches for my hand. "I think, my darling, Mr. Brower might realize we're here for more than just a tour of his lavish castle."

Brower narrows his eyes. "Why are you here?"

Chapter 9

Kimba

As Lance Brower's eyes bore into us, everything about Rey changes. He lifts his chin and straightens his back. "Fair enough." The sniveling persona is no more.

"As I mentioned this morning, my wife has had a difficult time. I'd like those difficulties to end. We're done with traveling and walking, with blisters and exhaustion. We're ready to stop, to find a place and settle in. We thought we'd be able to do that at the Dosen home. Jennifer made us all sorts of promises about the life we could build here. Now she's dead, and the boys—nice as they are—don't know what they're doing."

Lance leans forward in his chair. "That's obvious."

"Of course, I don't know anything about ranching either. But it's clear you do."

I watch as Brower swells with pride. Rey picks up on it, too, and gives him a nod. "Kim and I are here with a proposition."

I smile sweetly. While Rey may have switched from sniveler to self-assured, him calling me Kim clues me in to continue my weak-willed whiner routine, maybe even take it up a notch.

"Go on." Lance motions with his glass.

"I was thinking, if we stayed on, helped you keep the boys in line, it'd be beneficial for all of us."

Lance takes a slow sip of his drink. "Mm-mmm. That really hits the spot. The first sip's a burner, but after that, it's almost smooth. Sure you won't have some?"

I let out a breezy laugh. "It's been so long since I've had a drink, one sip would have me giggling."

"And that'd be bad? Let your hair down, relax."

"Maybe next time." Rey gives a dismissive wave. "Now, about my proposition . . ."

Lance takes another sip before smacking his lips. "What's in it for me?"

My husband lets out an exasperated sigh. "I help you with the Dosen boys."

"Here's the thing, friend, I don't *need* help with them. Their claim to the land is tenuous at best, especially considering the circumstances. Why, I doubt their daddy even had a will. Nope. Them showing up doesn't really change much."

"So you think things will just go on as they have been? They'll toe the line and do what you want?"

Lance gives Rey a hard look. "Is that what I said? I said, them being here doesn't change much. Truth be told, I don't really know if I have a place for the two of you. And Tara said there were a bunch of kids in your group. They belong to you?"

"Humph," I snort, motioning to my body. "Do I look like I have children?"

His eyes take me in. He raises his eyebrows. "Not at all. You're— "

Rey clears his throat. "Anyway, I think Kim and I would fit in nicely. We'll help you with the brothers and the others traveling with us. They know how to survive without anything. Like your cook, Twila was it? The ones in our group can make a meal out of a patch of weeds. It might take some of the load off your help if we start tending to the Dosen ranch."

"Thanks for your offer." Lance's eyes show the effects of the alcohol. "But I'll take a pass. Your best bet would be to hustle on back to the Double D and pack up. Those Dosens were nothing but trouble 'fore the lights went out. I'm not interested in working with them now."

"What do you mean?" I ask, leaning forward in my chair.

His eyes travel to the tank top I'm wearing under my long-sleeved shirt. I made sure to undo the top four buttons.

"He means he's going to send his henchmen to kill the boys," Rey says.

I put a hand to my mouth and open my eyes wide. "You wouldn't."

Brower throws back his head and laughs, sounding something like a turkey. Once he has himself composed, he quickly stands, pushing the chair into the wall behind him.

I feel my body tense, expecting an attack. I relax slightly when I realize he's just going after another drink.

I started training in jiujitsu when I was in college. My martial arts training was advanced and became more so during my time working for the government. When Rey and I started our consulting firm, I stayed with my training, on a less-intense level, until a few weeks before Nicole was born. Then I took a break.

Rey did most of the field work for our business, and I stayed at home doing the paperwork side of things and taking care of the children. The rare job we took needing my particular prowess, we made sure were low on the danger scale. By then, I was more of a soccer mom as opposed to a secret agent.

After the attacks and making our way to Bakerville, where we ran into my old friend, the training started again. We kept it up during our travels, making sure everyone in our group could defend themselves. It's helped more than once. I can't say my skills would impress any true black belts, but I give it all I've got, knowing my life may depend on it. And if I can get to my knife, then I really shine.

Rey lightly clears his throat. When I look toward him, he raises one eyebrow and lifts a finger. I answer with a smile. I don't know exactly what he has in mind, but his motions indicate he's going to make a move. I need to be ready.

Lance stumbles back to his chair, plops himself down, and lets out a boozy breath. "Where were we? Oh, yes, we were to the point of wrapping this up. You folks need to head on home, pack up, and get out."

Rey leans forward. "Or else?"

"Take it however you want. Stay, go—I don't much care."

"Because you won't be dirtying your hands with us anyway? You'll send someone else to do it. Not EJ Martin, though. He's not involved with the killing, is he? No, it's the rest of them, the ones you brought on after the lights went out. You don't have the stomach to do it yourself, don't have the guts. You're happy to have others do your dirty work, happy to delegate."

I look at Rey, my face registering as much shock as I can muster. "Now, honey, you shouldn't talk to Mr. Brower like that."

Brower slams a hand on his desk. "Listen to the woman. She's obviously the only one with brains. Why, I could kill you right here and not bat an eye."

"*You* could kill me? Or you'd call your gang? Maybe your son Declan? Let him prove himself to you? Or how about the other one?

What'd you say his name is? He's a disappointment to you, right? Him killing us, maybe that'd go a long way toward earning some respect."

Lance visibly swallows. He leans forward, spilling some of his drink. "I snap my fingers and *poof.* That's it for you," he slurs.

Rey leans back in his chair, knitting his hands behind his head. "Yeah, well, how about this? How about, instead of sending the others to do your dirty work, you lead the charge? Show us what you're really made of."

"Oh, I will. You—the whole lot of you—had better be gone by noon tomorrow. Because I'm coming for you. A whiny little nobody like you isn't going to . . . you can't come into my home and think you can threaten me. Now get out. Get gone. Or get dead."

Rey stands. "If that's the way you want it. Kim, let's go."

"Wait. Just wait." I lift my hands in the air. "I think . . . things have gone terribly wrong here. Mr. Brower, we just came to make a deal."

"He's not interested in deals." Rey holds his hand out to me. "Our time here is done. You heard him, we have until noon tomorrow to get out, or he's coming after us." Rey looks back to Brower. "Him— he's doing it. He isn't just sending his crew."

"That's right." Brower's eyes are unfocused, but his jaw is tight. "I'm coming after you. Noon tomorrow."

"I'll believe it when I see it. I still say you don't have the guts."

I turn to Rey. "Stop. You're making things worse. I want to stay here. I'm done traveling." I turn to Brower. "Please. Please, Mr. Brower. We'll . . . let us— "

"Now, Kim." Rey pulls on my hand. "We're leaving."

I drop my chin to my chest. "I am so done with this."

"Noon tomorrow." Brower points as we leave the room. "Noon. Be gone or be dead."

Once we're out of his sight, we move quickly to the front door.

Tara Brower is standing off the foyer in the living room. She smirks and runs her finger across her throat. "Noon tomorrow."

Rey hustles me out the front door. "Count them as we go," he whispers.

As we speed walk to the gravel two-track road, I focus on the people—the men working and standing around, a woman in the garden, her chin held high. Martin, the foreman, sees us and lifts a hand. I'm half surprised when he instructs the guy who took Rey's gun to give it back.

Once we reach the paved state road, Rey says, "How many you get?"

"Fourteen."

"I got twelve. Scott said there are two dozen. Did you count EJ Martin?"

"No, not him. Like you said, he won't be part of the raid. And there's no way Brower will wait until noon tomorrow."

"Nope, not a chance. My guess is he'll have another drink or two and then call for his main killer."

"I think I saw him, his killer, when we were waiting by the pickup. He was over to the right with a carbine."

Rey scrunches his face. "Red ballcap?"

"That's the one."

"Could be." Rey nods. "They'll raid just before dawn."

I let out a sigh. "Why is it always at dawn? The most beautiful part of the day shouldn't be ruined by gunfire."

"And no way will Brower be with them. He'll be home, either still snug in his bed or pacing his study. I couldn't get a read on which way he'd go."

"His son said he waits in his study. He'll be pacing. He wants to be part of the action but knows he's a weak, liver-bellied coward."

"Weak, liver-bellied coward? I think you have your metaphors combined."

"You want to take the fight to him? Attack Brower while the crew is gone? I saw you checking out the lock on the door."

"Not much of a lock. I may not even need my kit for it."

Rey's kit is a small lock picking set. Part of his everyday carry, it looks like a credit card with three specialty tools for getting into most places. When we left our home, he grabbed a small bag with a slightly larger tool collection and a few other things we thought might be useful.

"So, you want to go to him?"

"That's what I'm thinking."

I shake my head. "I think we do what he said. Leave."

"Atticus and Axel will never go for it."

"Convince them. Tell them they need to. Did you get a look at your twelve? Because I wasn't just counting, I was looking. And I saw evil. Pure evil."

He reaches for my hand. "Lower your voice."

I yank my arm away. "I am not going to let another one of my children die, or anyone else I love, because we made another foolish decision."

"Kimba. Lower. Your. Voice. You know how sound can travel."

"No," I hiss. "They'll just think it's part of the show anyway. Who cares if they hear? They'll know I want to leave." I manage to keep my voice at a normal level, though what I want is to scream at him, to yell and tell him how stupid we've been.

"Okay. That's a good point. But . . ." Rey lifts his hand. "I can't convince Atticus and Axel to leave. And I'm not even sure I should. Lance Brower is part of the evil you saw—the leader of it. He may put on an act of being a good old boy, but he isn't. He's a blight on this entire area. He needs to be stopped."

"And then what? You think it'll end with him? There're hundreds, *thousands*, more Lance Browers. Are you going to kill them all?"

I huff out a breath when Rey stops walking. He waits until I'm facing him before reaching for both of my hands. I yank my hands away.

A look of hurt changes his demeanor. "I'll kill any of them that are a threat to our family or friends."

I drop my gaze to the ground. "Even if it means more of us may die? If our daughters are killed?"

"I'll do whatever possible to prevent any more deaths." He touches a finger to my chin. "Look at me."

I shake my head. "I'm so . . . done."

"Kimba." He lowers his head until he's looking into my eyes, his gaze filled with pure love. "I know you. You don't want to let this . . . this . . ."

"Maggot?" I offer with a slight smile, feeling a connection with my husband for the first time in a long while.

"Maggot." He nods. "You don't want to let him keep terrorizing. He may have already wiped out everyone in the area. You heard Scott. Brower's taking over ranches between here and Augusta. How long do you think that'll be enough for him? How long until he grows his crew large enough he can take over the town of Simms?"

"And then what? You and I both know there's going to be another Lance somewhere down the road. Lance Brower, Jon Dawson, Richard Majors . . . they're all cut from the same cloth."

"It's the world we live in. As I said, if they're a threat to our family or our friends, we deal with them. We do it in a way that keeps Nicole and Naomi safe."

"You have a plan as to how to do that?"

"I like your idea. Go after Brower in his home."

Chapter 10

Nicole

"What do you think, Nicole? Does this look good?" Axel points to the line of wire he strung between two trees. "Should put them smack on their face?"

I wrinkle my nose. "Seems the right height. And with this being the first one, they won't expect it."

"I still think we should put the spiderweb out first." Axel wags his eyebrows. "Really show them we mean business."

"But then they'll know we've set traps. This way— " I motion toward the trip wire " —they might think their guy is just clumsy and fell over his own feet."

"Or how about we not mess with these things? Instead, we use deadly traps . . . not these namby-pamby things that do little more than slow them down and make them mad."

What a choice of words. Namby-pamby isn't a phrase I'd ever heard until meeting Jennifer Dosen. She had all sorts of unusual sayings and obscure expressions. A sharpness fills my chest. Jennifer's dead.

"Nicole's right," Victoria says. "We set up this one. It'll trip the first guy in line, and he'll go down. When the fishing line breaks, they won't even see the ends of it and will think he tripped over his own feet. After the second time, they'll realize they aren't just klutzes. Then we can start showing it's deliberate. Maybe the third is your snare or spiderweb."

"Of course," Jameson says, motioning with his hand, "this all is assuming they're going to use this trail along the river when they attack."

Axel nods. "They should, right? With the trees, we can't see them from the house. It makes more sense than just walking up the road in broad daylight."

"They'll probably attack when it's dark," I say. "Or at least get into position then."

Axel rolls his eyes. "You know what I meant."

I quickly turn away to hide my smile. It's way too easy to pick on Axel. He's a year younger than me, sixteen, but sometimes acts like he's Naomi's age. He tries to be all grown up and mature like Atticus, but the maturity level between them is amazing.

It's easy to see Axel's the youngest of the family. He's definitely a little on the spoiled side. Not the way Jameson was, all disrespectful and almost abusive, but definitely immature. I like him fine, but when he gets something in his head, he doesn't shut up about it. These traps, which he wishes were set up to not only slow the attackers down but to kill them, is one example.

He also keeps talking about going back to Simms and joining the hunting party to get the bear that killed his mom. I get it. When someone you love dies, you want to see justice done. Killing the bear could give him justice . . . and closure.

It's not the same for my family. How do you get revenge against the wind? Maybe in the way my mom is trying to, by blaming God? She doesn't say much about it, but I know she does. She's stopped praying, stopped reading the Bible, stopped all of it.

Things are like they used to be before we moved to Bakerville. In the past, we'd go to church a few times a year when something big was happening: a special service or a concert. Wow, that was some church. Thousands attended. They'd have famous Christian singers and speakers perform on a regular basis, and they'd sell tickets to big events.

Once in a while, I'd go to youth group activities. But we were never regular. And we certainly didn't read the Bible or pray at home. I didn't even own a Bible. I didn't think my parents did either, but my dad says he had one in a bedroom drawer that someone in the men's group of the mega church gave him. It was still brand new, the spine uncracked.

My dad seems to be going back to God. A few nights ago, when Atticus was reading the Bible, Dad spoke up for the first time since Nate died. The things he said made me cry. I could see how we'd been going along in a fog, relying on our own way to get us out of our grief, but it wasn't happening. We need to find God again. Find the comfort He offers. Find the love He offers.

If we don't . . . I'm not sure what'll happen. My mom's losing it. She's not the same as she used to be. She's gone soft. If she doesn't want to continue with the plans we made, plans to help put our country back together, I'm going on my own. I'll leave them all and—

"Well," Victoria says, bringing me back to the present, "let's get these things done. It's hotter than the devil along this river. You'd think the shade of the trees would help cool it down. And the bugs. Ugh."

"It's the humidity," Brett says. "I swear I can see the steam rising off the water."

"Won't be long and we'll be wishing for the heat of summer," Axel says. "It gets plenty cold here in the winter. If Atticus was with us, he'd tell you. Our dad used to talk about a winter when he was a kid, saying our grandpa threw his coffee in the air and it froze before it hit the ground."

I snort out a laugh. "Ya think?"

"Last winter was too cold." Jameson gives a fake shiver. "And too much snow. No way this year can be as bad. It was nuclear winter, right? And that should be gone now since we're having a normal summer."

"Is it normal?" Axel asks. "We had more rain than I ever remember. Even now, it's not as hot as it could be—as it *should* be even."

"Whatever, dude." Jameson waves him off. "Let's just get this done, set up the traps and put out the noisemakers closer to the house. I hope Atticus and Scott are getting their stuff finished. 'Course, Scott'll probably run to Brower and snitch about everything and it won't matter anyway."

Axel vigorously shakes his head. "I don't believe that. Scott's no snitch."

"Correction. Scott *wasn't* a snitch. A lot has changed in the last year. Seems Scott's pretty comfortable with the way things are."

Axel's face pales at Jameson's words. "Let's just get this done."

Chapter 11

Kimba

Patti's in the yard of the smaller house, her long black hair in double braids hanging down each shoulder. She's wearing an oversized salmon colored T-shirt from Nina's closet over her usual lightweight hiking pants. The shirt is a wonderful complement to her warm brown skin.

At twenty-three, she's a beautiful young woman and seemingly unmarred by the tragedies of the past year. Even the loss of her husband, though she grieves deeply, hasn't dimmed the light she carries within.

I close my eyes and take a breath. I wish I could say the same. Since Nate died, I've changed. Not just inside, where part of me died that night too, but externally. I may have turned Lance Brower's head, but I'm not nearly as attractive as I once was.

I flex the muscles in my back. My looks may be fading, but I'm in the best shape of my life. After Nate died, exercise kept me from totally losing my mind. I'd punish my body for hours on end, running wind sprints, lifting boulders and logs, or sparring with anyone who was foolish enough to take me on.

"Hey." Patti swipes the back of her hand across her forehead. "How'd it go?"

"About as expected." Rey bends down to look at the string of cans Patti's working on. "Where'd you find these?"

"The sheds. You wouldn't believe all the stuff they have stashed. Typical ranchers."

I tilt my head to the side. "Meaning?"

"I'm pretty sure they've never thrown anything away, including these rusted soup cans. We also found bottles, pop cans, and even a whole bunch of large sleigh bells. The boys are putting them out in various places."

"Noisemakers everywhere." Rey nods. "That's good, even if they are a little primitive."

Patti steps closer to us and lowers her voice. "That's not all. We tried to keep our preparations a secret, without letting Scott find out.

Unfortunately, he met up with Atticus in one of the sheds and seemed to realize right away that we were working on an alarm system. He said it was a great idea."

Rey shakes his head. "I guess it couldn't be helped. Did he say anything else?"

"Not as far as I know, but he's with Atticus now."

"What!" I exclaim. "He'll know where the traps are. He could tell Brower."

She screws up her face. "I don't think he will. I think he's tired of being under Brower's thumb and thinks part of the troubles with his fiancée is her dad. If Brower wasn't in the picture, they could start fresh."

"Doubt that."

Patti pinches her forehead. "The little we saw of her last night, I'd have to agree. She's a daddy's girl through and through. Anyway, I was thinking, how do you feel about a pit trap?"

"Pit trap?" I shake my head. "We don't want to set up anything that can harm one of us."

"I know, and we'd need to be careful, but the ground's plenty soft here. It'd take about as long as digging— " She takes in a noisy breath. "As long as the grave took to dig. If we put one on the trails, it'd at least give us one less threat. Speaking of, was Scott right about there being two dozen?"

We give a brief account of what we learned, not going into details of our plan. We'll save those for when everyone's together. Patti assures us the rest of our group should be back shortly, and if we want to move forward with a pit trap or two, we'd better get to digging.

I like the idea of trapping a few of the bad guys, but I don't like that Scott knows our every move. And no way could we prevent him from seeing us dig a trap, not on this open ranch land.

"How are the children?" I ask.

"They're in the basement. Axel showed up with a stash of dusty toys he cleaned up for them to play with. Naomi and LJ were ecstatic. I'm sure Trish is ready for something to eat, so I'd better go check on them."

Rey spends a few minutes looking over the alert Patti was working on: old soup cans filled with rocks, then a lid made out of duct tape. She punched a hole in each can and ran a length of twine through it. Like Rey said, it's primitive but is better than nothing.

"That should work," I say. "What do we have for a trip wire?"

"Fishing line maybe? The boys probably took it with them."

Within a few minutes, Atticus appears with Scott by his side. The hired man shakes hands with the teen before heading to the big house.

"Axel back?" Atticus asks as he approaches.

"I don't think so," Rey responds. "We've only been here ten minutes or so. Patti didn't mention him being here. Are Nicole and Brett with him?"

"And Victoria."

I shake my head. "I hope there isn't any trouble."

"There they are." Rey points toward the river, where Victoria's stepping from a scraggly brush. "Why the river? It'll be hard to hear the alarms from there, especially ones like this." He motions to the string of cans.

"We found some primers in my dad's reloading stuff. Those should be loud enough. And, uh . . . well, we thought we'd add a few things out of Scott's view to slow them down."

"Such as?"

"Nothing lethal, don't want anyone stumbling on them by mistake, or the cattle or deer. A few snares and stronger trip wires, the kind that'll take them down and land them splat on their faces. And we had a cargo net in one of the sheds. Axel was going to set it up as a trap."

Rey's quiet, unmoving.

Atticus looks toward him, a question in his eyes.

In a slow, monotone voice, Rey says, "You do understand we will kill anyone—*everyone*—who attacks us."

I watch Atticus's face, looking for him to balk, to flinch.

He lifts his chin. "I know. But we need to be sure of who we're killing and not just setting out some indiscriminate device that takes out everyone and everything."

Rey's mouth forms a slight smile. "And Scott doesn't know?"

"About the traps? Nope. They took simple noisemakers with them, part of the ploy. Scott and I put out most of them. We used the cattle and game trails, thinking that's how Brower's men will come in. We also put a few on the hillside behind us, all close enough we should hear. Looks like Patti finished another."

"Good thinking on the snares and stuff."

Atticus gives a nod and then asks about our visit with Brower.

"He was surprisingly cordial," I say. "At first."

"Bet he was. Did he give you the grand tour? House and stables?"

"Only the house. Things took a turn before we got the outside tour. And he was a little drunk, so . . ." I lift my hands as I shrug.

"Figures. When Scott was talking about him stocking the town with booze, I knew he kept plenty for himself. Did he show you his wine cellar?"

"Is it in the basement? We didn't go down there."

"Yeah. He had quite a collection, made wine and stuff then too. All his setups were electric. Maybe his backup solar is strong enough to keep them going?"

"Well, I guess a man has priorities." I wink at Atticus.

He throws his head back. "I suppose so. Still, it's interesting."

"Isn't it?" Rey smirks. "What about Scott?"

Atticus shakes his head. "Not much we could do to keep him in the dark. He's afraid of Brower."

"Of Brower, or his hired guns?"

"Good point. He kept talking about the Laubin family and others he'd heard about who met the same fate. He thinks we should leave. That when the noisemakers go off, we should skedaddle."

"Skedaddle?" I ask with a smile.

"I've been thinking . . . he might be right."

"Oh?" I ask, shooting Rey a look.

"This isn't your fight, and it isn't Patti's or Victoria's either. It's my fight. Axel's, too, if he insists. The rest of you should go."

"We won't leave you." Rey's voice is determined and final. "The others are almost here. We'll talk inside."

After everyone takes a few minutes to get water and settle in, with the three youngest in the basement napping, Rey says it's time to make our plan. He starts by giving an overview of our visit to Brower's ranch, including what we know about the household staff and the ranch hands.

"No way EJ Martin would be involved with the stuff Brower does to take over other ranches," Axel says.

"We directly asked, and Brower agreed. Martin's the foreman of the ranch but not one of the raiders."

"But the rest?"

"We should assume they do their boss's bidding."

"That's about two to one?"

"We saw fourteen," I say. "There's undoubtedly more. Scott said two dozen."

There're several beats of silence before Victoria says, "I'm in. I'll do whatever you need. It's only right. Jennifer would've fought. I'll fight in her place."

A mumble of agreement goes through the group. I shake my head. "I'm against this. Rey knows I am."

"Mom!" Nicole gasps.

I look to Atticus. "You know I love you, Axel too. I just can't stand losing anyone else. Your mom and— " my voice catches " —Nate, their deaths were accidents. Asher, though, he was murdered."

"My mom was murdered." Axel leans forward. "That bear murdered her."

"Fair enough." I nod. "Point is, I don't want to lose anyone else."

Rey reaches for my hand.

I reluctantly allow him to take it, leaving it like a limp fish.

He gives it a slight squeeze. "Atticus and Axel deserve our help with this."

I purse my lips and take a breath, winding up for an explosion of words.

Rey squeezes my hand again. "That said, Kimba's right. We know Brower's men slaughtered an entire family."

"More than one, from what Scott said." Atticus leans toward me. "Look, Kimba, I'm with you. I don't want anyone hurt. I told you earlier, I'll stand alone."

"Just walk away. Move into Simms. You can get your land back later."

"Can I? And if it was your place, would you?"

"If it meant keeping my children safe, yes."

"We're going to keep the children safe," Rey says. "You know that, love. Here's what I'm thinking. Like we discussed, we go to him. When his hoodlums are coming here to attack, we're there, waiting and watching for him to leave. The children will be hidden safely away."

"Safe where?" I ask.

"I know a place," Atticus says. "The fort we used to play in. Well, not really a fort . . . it's a natural structure, but it's hidden. It's along the ridgeline on the east side of the property. There's a rock outcropping along the front, giving a good vantage point. One side is closed in from the scrub brush and trees. The other side has boulders and more brush, but the back is wide open, giving a place to get out—a secondary exit."

"Sounds pretty good." Rey rubs his chin. "Good views?"

"Perfect. Perched up on the edge, we can see all the way to the western fence line—the one that separates us from Brower."

"And an easy out at the back?" I say, confirming what he already said.

"Yep. The back is open. You'd be hidden, too, if you left out the back. As long as you stoop over, the rocks along the front and side will provide cover."

"What about Scott?"

"Let's lock him in the basement," Jameson offers.

I frown. "They'd kill him. If he's here or at the big house, he's a dead man."

"Agreed." Rey leans forward. "We'll find a place to stash him. Nicole, Patti, and Jameson will stay here with the children."

"Dad." Nicole presses her lips together.

"You're trained. Patti and Jameson don't have the same skills. Neither of them knows the defensive maneuvers you do. Jameson never trained with the militia."

Jameson crosses his arms. "I can keep the kids safe. Or I can go with you and do whatever you need."

"I know you can. What we need is you and Nicole helping Patti with her children and Naomi. I need to know Naomi is taken care of so I can do my job."

Lifting his chin, Jameson uncrosses his arms. "I'll do it."

"Thank you." Rey stands and moves to Jameson, reaching out to shake his hand. A tinge of pink reaches the youth's cheeks. Rey turns to our daughter. "Nicole?"

"Of course, Dad." He gives her a smile before she mutters, "I'm a good little soldier."

Rey lets out a breath. "Really, Nicole?"

She rolls her eyes. "I'll do what you want. And you know that if something happens to you and Mom, I'll take care of Naomi."

I send my daughter a grateful smile.

Rey opens his mouth in response but is interrupted by Axel. "And the rest of us?"

"We're going to Brower," I say. "We kill him—preferably silently—then take care of anyone who returns and still feels the need to fight."

"What about Connor? Mouth?"

"And Tara," Atticus adds.

"We'll keep them secured. Hopefully we can let them live."

I glance to Rey for confirmation. "If we can, we will. Um, one other thing . . ." He lets out a long breath. "You're not going. You'll be with Nicole and the children."

Chapter 12

Kimba

"No. No, that's not happening." I yank my hand from Rey's grasp. "I'm not being sidelined."

"You aren't being sidelined, Kimba. This is where you're needed."

I cross my arms and narrow my eyes. "Really? I'm needed here, hiding out?"

"We don't know what they'll do. You saw those guys. Whatever we think they might do, it doesn't mean much. Most aren't trained for this, but they do enjoy it."

Pursing my lips, my eyes shoot to Nicole. The look on her face . . . relief? Hope? Whatever it is, it gives me pause. I drop my gaze and silently exhale.

One, two, three, four . . .

My shoulders soften. I inhale four breaths, then turn to my husband. "What are you thinking?"

I feel the tension in the room lessen as everyone seems to release their own collective breaths. I've noticed it—the way they walk on eggshells around me since Nate died, never sure if I'm going to burst out in tears or snap at one of them. I try not to be like this, but it's there. The way I've changed, the way I'm more like the persona I was pretending to be with Brower than I want to admit.

Weak. Sniveling. A trainwreck.

I can't even keep myself together the way I should. My chest starts to tighten, the hint of a panic attack coming on. I concentrate on my breathing as the conversation continues around me.

Rey leans forward and meets Atticus's gaze. "Where's your old fort?"

"Top of the hill, near the road. You can see the rocks from here, but nothing else. You'll have to go up there to see what it looks like."

I give a single dip of my head. Rocks not only help with concealment but also provide cover if there's any shooting. And he said there's an opening on the back of it to give us a way out if things go bad. That's important.

"All right. Let's put one of Patti's pit ideas somewhere on the way there, too, just in case it's not as hidden as we think."

"We're back to the trouble with Scott," Atticus says. "What will we do with him?"

Axel reaches a hand to the back of his neck, twisting his head slightly. "I think we can trust him. I *want* to trust him."

Rey steeples his hands, his index fingers touching the tip of his chin. "We all want to trust him. But we can't risk it."

"I have an idea." Axel looks to his older brother. "Maybe . . . how about the blind we built?"

"What kind of blind?" Rey also turns to Atticus.

"It's not much. A bunch of twigs and branches we put up in kind of a teepee." He glances to Patti. "Um, not really a teepee, just that shape."

She gives him a smile and motions with her hands for him to go on.

"Uh, so, we'd have to tie him up, gag him. And I suppose someone would need to stay with him."

I shake my head. "We'd be better off securing him and keeping him with me. Jameson or Nicole could keep a bead on him."

"True," Rey agrees. "Keeping everyone together is our best choice. I'll take Atticus, Axel, and Brett with me."

Victoria lets out a slight gasp. She quickly recovers before saying, "I'll go with you."

Raising a hand, he shakes his head. "I know you're willing, but you don't have the training. It makes sense for you to stay so you can help watch Scott and keep the kids safe and quiet. You'll need to use the rifle, okay?"

Victoria scrunches her face before giving a determined nod.

"Brower told Scott he should spend the night at his house with Tara," Atticus reminds us.

"Yep." Rey runs his tongue along his teeth, puffing out his upper lip before making a clicking noise with his tongue. "It'd be better if he did."

Axel squares his shoulders. "And what will we do?"

"We'll wait until they leave and then go in quiet. Brett'll be overwatch, staying somewhere with a good view of everything. One of you will make sure the staff stays in the basement. One will be on the second floor, keeping Brower's children—and possibly Scott—out of the way. I'll take care of Brower."

"Will four be enough?" I ask.

"It'll have to be."

"I could go too," Jameson says again.

"Or me," Nicole offers. "If Mom's here, she'll be able to take care of Naomi."

My heart pounds in my chest. Nicole is well trained from her time on the Bakerville militia, but I don't want her there. I want her hidden away and out of danger.

"Um, I was wondering something." Patti raises her hand.

"Yes?" Rey asks.

"Do you think they're watching us? Maybe he sent spies?"

I meet Rey's eyes, and my mouth goes in an *O* shape. Are we really so out of it we didn't consider this?

"Why do you ask?" Rey leans toward the younger woman.

Her lips go in a tight line. "Just a feeling. Earlier, when I was outside working on the string of cans, I kept getting the feeling I was being watched. But I never saw anyone."

Axel and those who set up the booby traps along the river say they didn't see anyone either. Atticus agrees. I think back to when Rey and I returned from Brower's. We took the main road. Nothing seemed out of the ordinary.

Rey leans back in his chair. "It's a good point. Where would they set up?"

Atticus and Axel share a look before shaking their heads. They both start to speak. Axel motions for Atticus to go ahead.

"You can see what it's like between here and Brower's place— gentle, rolling hills and flat pastures. I suppose the larger hill, the one right on the property line, would give a good view. They'd see plenty if they had strong binoculars. And if they're lying prone, we might not notice them. Other than that— "

"Along the river," Axel jumps in. "We were there and didn't see anything." He looks to Nicole and Brett, who both agree. "But if they used the river trail and then circled around to our fort, that'd be the perfect spot."

"Which is why I suggested it," Atticus says. "It has a good view of the entire ranch and is well hidden from here."

"Can we see the place from here?" Rey asks.

Atticus tilts his head to the side. "The office would have the best view. Maybe the master bedroom too."

"You and your brother each take a room. Scan the entire area with your binoculars. Kimba, you and Brett scan the line of trees along the river. Look for any movement or anything out of the ordinary. I'll take the property line hill."

We spend over half an hour glassing the area, searching for anything that doesn't belong. About halfway through, Rey has us switch locations to put fresh eyes in each spot. When we're somewhat satisfied there isn't anyone watching, we meet back in the living room. The babies and Naomi are now awake from their naps and are sitting with us.

"I'm going up to the fort," Rey says. "Atticus, Kimba, cover me from the house windows. Axel, you'll come with me, but stop partway to provide cover and watch for any movement. We'll use the click system on the radio to communicate."

"Yes, sir." Axel puffs out his chest.

"Once we know it's clear, I'll walk the river. You'll reposition and use the ranch house for cover so there are no blind spots. Axel will be my wingman again."

"We've got the traps set up on the river," Atticus cautions. "You don't want to walk the path."

"Good point. Did you only set things up on the obvious path?"

Atticus looks to his younger brother, who lifts a shoulder. "Yeah. Seemed like the way they'd go since there are so many trees. Was it wrong?"

"Nope," Rey answers. "They'll probably take the easiest route. I'll walk the edge of the trees."

"If someone is watching, they'll know we're on to them," I say.

Rey shakes his head. "It can't be helped."

"What about the property line?" Axel asks. "Do the same with it?"

Atticus wrinkles his forehead. "There's no one up there. We would've found them when we were glassing."

"We'll walk it anyway," Rey responds. "We need to get a move on. We're about four hours from sunset."

"And you think they'll attack at dawn?" There's a quiver in Victoria's voice. "Not before then?"

"That's assuming several things, like the popularity of attacking at dawn. Brower probably watched movies that showed it."

"The other family was attacked at dawn," Jameson says. "Scott said it was right around sunup when the fire started."

"It's not just in movies." I give my husband a pointed look. "Historically, there've been many predawn attacks. The attackers move into place under the cover of darkness, in hopes of catching the enemy still sleeping or at least groggy as the sunrises. And if they position themselves to the east, they have an even bigger advantage."

"Correct," Rey agrees. "Which is why the fort is so appealing—not only for our use but for their use too. Get snacks if you need them, and make sure your water bottles are full." He turns to Victoria. "Were you able to refill our water?"

"They have a narrow well bucket set up to retrieve water. We still bleached it as a precaution. It should be ready for use."

"We had a bunch of chlorine tablets in the root cellar for shocking our well," Axel says. "They were still down there. I guess Brower didn't need them."

"Good thing," I say.

"Very good thing." Rey nods.

"Plenty of food here too," Patti says. "Looks like they may have taken unopened things but left a lot behind. I did a search of the pantry. Some of the dry goods have been infested."

"Infested?" I raise my eyebrows.

She lifts a shoulder. "Weevils."

A shudder runs through me as Nicole says, "Gross."

"They got into the white flour and white rice. We can rinse the rice and still use it."

"No way." Nicole is wide eyed, shaking her head.

Rey moves toward the door. "We'll worry about the bugs later. Refill your waters. Eat something and relax for a few minutes. Axel and I are leaving in fifteen."

The exploration of the surrounding area comes up clear. As I'm walking from a lookout position against the main ranch house while Rey and Axel finish with the property line, my eyes travel across to the land on the other side of the paved road.

My breath catches when I glimpse movement. Anger burns in the pit of my stomach. *Stupid. Stupid. Stupid.* I try to remain nonchalant as I continue toward the smaller house. Once I'm hidden in the shadow of the building, I rush inside.

"Nicole!" I call out.

She steps from the kitchen. "Yes?"

"We forgot about the area across the road. I need you in the front yard. Stay up against the house, out of sight, but make the intruder signal over and over until all of our people out there see it. Patti, get the children to the basement. Victoria, watch out the front window for our people to return. Holler when you see them, and tell me who it is."

"What's happening?" Atticus asks as he steps from the second bedroom, where he was using the binoculars to track Rey and Axel as they scout the area.

"We're stupid, that's what's happening." I slide into the office and use the same window as earlier when I watched the fort.

Atticus is right on my heels.

"This is no good." I move to the other window, staying toward the edge and out of sight.

Atticus moves to the other edge.

We stand in silence for several beats, scanning the area with our eyes until Atticus says, "There. I see him." He puts his binoculars up while giving me landmarks to look for.

Once I catch the movement, I put my binos up. There they are. Two men are on their stomachs, using the brush for concealment. They're dressed in desert colors—one holding a long rifle, his eye on the scope, while the other has binoculars in position. My breath catches.

"Are they— " Atticus's voice cracks.

"I'm not sure. They look set up to shoot, but . . ." I shake my head. "He might just be using the scope like binoculars."

"Jameson's almost here!" Victoria calls through the house. "He just rounded the edge of the big house. He, uh . . . he sees Nicole signaling. Does he know the signal?"

I look to Atticus, who answers with a shrug.

"Get his attention. Motion him to come inside."

"They see him," Atticus whispers. "The rifle guy just repositioned."

I grunt out a response as I move to the bottom of the partially open window and rest my rifle on the sill. The screen is still in place, which will help hide my movements. I can shoot through if needed, but the barrier prevents me from having a solid rest. I look at the two men through my scope, focusing on the potential shooter.

"He's not going to shoot. He's not." Atticus's voice is pleading. "Dear God, please don't let him shoot."

I relax when the guy drops the muzzle and lifts his eye from the scope. A stream of sweat starts in the middle of my back. "Atticus, find me something better for a rest, please."

He scrambles away from the window, taking care to stay out of sight, and quickly returns with a bar stool from the kitchen. It's slightly higher than the base of the window.

"Slow movement. They aren't looking this way, so don't give them a reason to."

The creak of the front door sounds through the house as Atticus puts the stool in position.

"Jameson's inside," Victoria announces.

"What's happening?" the boy asks his mother.

I don't hear her response, but seconds later she lets us know Brett is on his way back.

"Brett knows the signals," Atticus says. "If he sees Nicole, he'll know there's an intruder."

As before, the two on the hill catch sight of Brett and perk up.

I focus on my breathing, willing myself to be calm. *Breathe in for the count of four, hold for four, out through my mouth for eight.*

The men on the hill shift slightly.

Brett's not yet back when Victoria calls out, "Axel and Rey are together, still on the other side of the horse corral."

With Brett in the house, I tell Atticus, "Find someplace where Brett can provide cover fire if necessary, but he's not to shoot unless they shoot or he hears me shoot. And look out the front and make sure Nicole's okay." He runs off to do my bidding as I keep my focus on the infiltrators.

Atticus is back much quicker than I expect. "Rey got the signal. He and Axel put space between them. They're still heading this way, looking casual, but I know they know. And I took Brett to the master bedroom patio and hid him behind the air conditioner. They won't be able to see him from there, but he has a decent view, and the unit will make not only a good rest but also give him some protection. It'll be side shooting, but it should work to confuse them. Where do you want me?"

"With me. Get the other stool and set up at the other window. You should have a good view from there."

It's several long, tense minutes as we wait for Axel and Rey to return. I know they're getting close when I see the muzzle of the rifle drop again and the men start talking to each other.

I let out a long, calming breath. When the front door opens, I carefully move from my perch. "Keep watch. I'm talking to Rey."

Atticus grunts out his agreement.

"Where are they?" Rey asks when he sees me.

Victoria scurries past us, muttering about checking on the children and Patti in the basement.

I motion toward the office. "The hill across the road. We didn't— "

He runs his hands through his hair. "We missed them."

"Careless. We were careless. We haven't done things right since . . . since Nate. That's what I'm saying." My voice rises several octaves. "We have no business doing this. Our professionalism is gone. We're going to get someone killed."

Chapter 13

Kimba

Rey drops his head. In barely a whisper, he says, "Calm down."

"Calm down? Calm down? Do you— " I slam my mouth shut and grit my teeth. Angry fire burns in my stomach, up my chest. My vision narrows. I dig my nails into my palms.

"We made a mistake. *I* made a mistake." Rey lifts his hands, palms up. "Now we know. We deal with it."

I narrow my eyes. "Deal with it? We could've . . . Naomi. Nicole." He reaches for me. I step away. "This—this is what I was talking about. You think we should stay and fight. We're in no condition to fight. We've lost our edge."

His mouth is a tight line as he runs a hand through his hair. "We have."

"Um, guys?" Jameson's voice is timid.

Rey and I turn toward him.

"Uh, yeah." He blinks rapidly. "We know about them now, right? What do we do?"

I close my eyes and drop my shoulders. Jameson's right. Blame won't get us anywhere. And with them there, watching us, we can't even retreat—not safely. Blaming Rey, *blaming myself,* doesn't do us any good. "Eliminate the threat."

"Yeah, that's about it." Rey moves toward the living room. He acts like he's going to sit, stops part way, and takes up pacing.

I turn back to Jameson. "Will you relieve Atticus? Send him out here, please." I lean against the wall, still seething, angrier at Rey than I should be. I know this isn't his fault, not entirely, but it feels right to blame him.

When Atticus steps into the hallway, I lift my chin toward him. "Any change?"

"They're no longer prone. They moved farther back, sitting on their bottoms, eating and drinking. It's no wonder we didn't see them. They really blend in with the background where they are now."

"Didn't see them?"

"Rey had me scan across the road earlier. I should've done a better job checking, maybe even walked over there."

I drop my chin and scratch my arm while letting out a long breath through my nose. Okay, so . . . Rey may have had Atticus glass across the road, but *obviously* it wasn't enough. He still dropped the ball.

Rey sinks to the couch and motions Atticus to take one of the chairs. "If you'd gone over there . . ." He shakes his head. "Now we know they're there. We'll take care of them. Kimba? Join us?" He taps the couch next to him.

I choose the other recliner, facing Rey instead of sitting next to him. "Go on."

He gives me a long look before turning to Atticus. "How can we get to them without being seen?"

"The river. Follow it east, loop around, and go in behind them. We should be hidden by the brush they're in, but it might be difficult to go in silently."

"Maybe we can make a diversion?" I suggest.

Rey offers me a slight smile. "Good idea. Maybe wait for their relief, let these two head back. After they're gone, we take out the new ones."

"Kill them?" Atticus visibly swallows.

"I can't imagine it'd go any other way."

"Then it has to be you and me. Not Axel, Nicole, or the Dawsons."

"Agreed." Rey bobs his head. "Or Kimba and me."

Atticus clenches his jaw. "I can do it. Probably be best if she's here, in case something goes wrong."

Rey agrees. "Can we get from here to the trees without being seen?"

Scrunching up his face in thought, Atticus gives a slow shake of his head. "We could go from here to Scott's old place or maybe the bunkhouse. They'd see us going there, but then we might be able to sneak from those buildings to the trees along the river."

"You think?" I ask. "Where they're at— "

Atticus shakes his head. "You're right. I don't know how we could get to the trees without them seeing us."

I jump when the radio lets out a squelch followed by a click.

Rey rises from his seat. "Nicole. She's on the front porch. I told her to pull out her book and pretend to read." He moves to the window. "Scott's heading this way." Rey moves to the door, opens it slightly, and speaks to Nicole in a tone too low to hear. He looks back to me. "That's what she was alerting us to—Scott."

"You want the show?" I ask.

"Nothing excessive."

I circle my shoulders and drop my head slightly before leaning back in the chair and crossing my legs. I'm still wearing the revolver, hidden low in the belly band, and my hair's no longer loose but pulled into a ponytail.

"Ready?" Rey mouths.

I wave him off with one hand.

"Hello, Scott," Rey says, opening the door wide. "Something we can help you with?"

The men shake hands before Scott steps in, removing his cowboy hat and holding it with both hands. He looks nervous. "Is the girl keeping watch?"

"Nicole? Keeping watch? I thought she was reading a book."

"Uh, yeah. She has a book with her. Atticus." He gives the young man a nod. "Where's everyone else?"

"Oh, here and there." I hunch my shoulders, my voice light and airy. *Ugh.* I hate the way I sound.

"Mm-hmm. Don't know if you all are aware . . . you're being watched."

My hands go to my mouth and my eyes go wide. "Watched? By whom?"

He furrows his brow. "Brower's men, of course."

I make my mouth go into an *O* shape. "Of course, that . . . um, that . . . why?"

"Where are they?" Rey asks, going to the front window and peering out.

"Across the road. You'll need to go to one of the back windows." He motions with his hand. "I know you folks think you can put out those strings of cans to maybe give you some warning. But what then? By the time you hear them—*if* you hear them—they'll be on top of you."

"I think we'll be okay." Rey claps Scott on the shoulder. "We talked with Brower. Seems we have an understanding. Although, I'm not sure why he'd send someone to watch us."

"Lance Brower can't be trusted. Whatever agreement you *think* you've reached is on your part only. He'll tell you one thing and do the complete opposite."

"And you allow it." Atticus's eyes bore into the Double D's former hired man.

Scott works the hat between his hands. I'm impressed when he meets Atticus's gaze. "Yup. I've explained this. I get that you don't understand. I did what I thought was best so your family might have a ranch to come home to. I admit, in hindsight, it was a mistake."

"Ya think?" Atticus says. "Why don't you man up and help us with Brower instead of telling us to run away?"

"Because I don't want to see you killed! Don't you get it? You'll end up just like Charley and the rest. Brower's men, they have no remorse. They'll kill you and your brother, the girl on the front porch, the babies." Scott's voice catches. "All of you."

My eyes search out Rey, and he answers with a barely perceptible shake of his head. I fluff my hair. "I'm sure we'll be fine."

"You say we're being watched," Rey says, "but it makes no sense. I told you, Brower— "

"And I told you, don't trust him. They probably have their radios and are reporting back to Brower's ranch."

"Radio?" I raise my eyebrows. "They have radios?"

"Yup. Similar to the ones you all have."

I respond with a smile while my mind whirls. This guy doesn't miss much. When we arrived, Rey used the radio to tell Patti it was safe. He thought he'd been discreet and kept it hidden. Maybe he saw the one Nicole has?

However he found out, it's another strike against us if Brower knows. It's also possible Scott has his own radio and realizes we're lying about reaching an understanding with Brower. The man could've called him as soon as we left, told him about the entire conversation. Scott could be playing both sides.

Rey crosses his arms. "Are you accepting Brower's invitation to stay there tonight?"

Scott plops his well-worn hat back on his head. "Guess I will. You folks won't listen to reason. I don't want to be here when the— " He clears his throat. "You might think you reached a deal, and I truly hope you did. Atticus, I've known you and Axel too long to stand by and watch you be murdered."

"Stand with us." Atticus gives Scott a hard look. "You know what's happening is wrong."

Scott's mouth goes into a tight line. "I won't fight Lance. He's Tara's dad—my fiancée's dad. If I fight him, what do you think it'd do to her? I wish you well, I truly do."

He looks like he wants to say more. Instead, he gives a shake of his head before telling us goodbye and pulling the door firmly closed.

Chapter 14

Nicole

"Miss Nicole." Scott gives me a nod as he exits the house.

I lift my chin at him, making sure my book is in full view.

His eyes go to it. He licks his lips and then shakes his head. "You folks are biting off more than you can chew."

I give what I hope is a serene smile.

"Yep." He shakes his head again. "More than you can chew. You're old enough you could take those kids and skedaddle, at least give them a chance. How're you related to them anyway?"

"Related?" I scramble to remember what Mom said I should say after she told Brower she didn't have children. "We're orphans, my sister and me. They took us in."

"That right? You sure look a lot like Kim. Same eyes. Same hair. 'Course, you've got the same coloring as Atticus and Axel too. You all could be family."

I lift a shoulder. "Comes in handy sometimes."

"Mm-hmm. I'd imagine. Think about what I said. You don't need to do this. None of you do. Talk to Atticus and Axel, tell them they've sacrificed enough."

"Okay." I look back at my book.

He lets out a noisy breath and then walks away.

The front door opens with a squeak. My dad pops his head out. "Nicole? C'mon in."

Inside the house, Dad stands at the front window. "He's heading to the barn."

Atticus makes a noise of disgust. "Probably getting his horse. Guess we won't have to tie him up and have Kimba watch him. He'll be with Tara. Does that change things?"

My dad looks to my mom. "We need another person."

Mom's eyes travel to me. She looks at the floor and releases a breath through her nose. She's counting, a thing she does to keep calm. When she finally speaks, she sounds defeated. "Nicole has the training.

Jameson doesn't." Her eyes meet mine. Her voice is barely a whisper. "Think you're ready?"

My stomach tightens as I give a crisp bob of my head. "I'll be with Dad. I'll be fine."

Dad visibly swallows. "Yes, you'll be fine. It's going to be a long night. Atticus and I will get in position to take out the watchers shortly after shift change."

"It'll need to be quick," Mom says. "If they have radios, you can't risk one of them calling."

"At the same time?" Atticus asks. "Take them out together?"

Dad nods. "Yup. Kimba, you're in charge of the diversion."

"Something loud but not too loud?"

"We have fireworks."

All eyes dart to Atticus.

"What kind?" Mom asks as Atticus bobs his head.

"All sorts. Bought a bunch before the last Fourth of July—before everything fell apart—but it was too dry to set them off. Planned on doing some for New Year's but didn't."

"Where are they?"

"In the basement of the main house, unless Brower took them."

Fireworks kept in the basement of a house . . . doesn't seem like the smartest place to store them.

"Scott has his horse ready," Dad says from the window. "He tied him to the rail and is heading back to the house."

"Maybe I should go over there now? Tell him we're going to use the fireworks as part of our warning system?" Atticus starts toward the door.

"He'll tell Brower," I say.

My dad lifts a shoulder. "Possibly, but that won't matter. And it'll make more sense if the guys watching see Atticus go in the house with Scott. Let's do it. Put the fireworks in something so our friends across the road don't know what you bring out."

"Yes, sir," Atticus agrees with a nod.

After he leaves, Dad asks my mom, "What time you think they'll have shift change?"

She crinkles her nose. "It's been about forty-five minutes since I first saw them. No idea how long they were there before that."

"Four, maybe six-hour shifts?"

"Four. In this heat, I'd say four."

"My thought too. We need to get a move on."

"This will be an all-nighter. How do you want to go about it? Try and get some naps in?"

"Patti's downstairs with the children?"

Mom nods. "Yes. I think Victoria went down there, too, after you and Axel came back."

Dad looks to me. "Brett and Nicole will both need to be sharp. Atticus had some operator training while we were on the security team, so he'll know what to do to stay alert."

The security team was a specially trained group in the Bakerville militia. It was mostly comprised of former military and law enforcement or people like my parents with extra training. Atticus, without any special training, earned a spot on the team through hard work.

"He'll be fine," my dad says, his voice sounding less than convincing. "Kimba, are you— "

"Psh." Mom lets out a snort. "I'm a trained operator, just like you."

"It's been a while."

She lifts her chin, looking strong and confident, the way she used to be before Nate died. "I'll be fine. When will you want me to let the fireworks off?"

"After the shift change and the two watching us now are out of sight and out of hearing. I'll click the radio to let you know when the shift change has happened." He turns from the window. "Atticus is on his way back."

Mom glances around the room. "I think we should send a whole group to the woods. Take a string of noisemakers along . . . a few other things. Then everyone comes back one or two at a time. Except you and Atticus."

"Hoping they can't count?"

"That's my hope."

"Let's do it." Dad looks at me with a nod. "Brett and Nicole will come back first. Have them try and nap. Patti stays here with the children. Naomi can watch the babies in the basement while Patti's in the office, keeping eyes on the guys across the road."

My mom's confident look deflates. She gives Dad a grim nod. Scott may be right; this might be too much for us. If my mom was how she used to be, ferocious and determined, we might stand a chance. But with the way she is now . . . I don't know.

My dad is only one person. Atticus had good training with the security team, but only for a few months. I was part of the militia, as were Brett and Axel, but most of our duties were standing guard—watching for threats and calling for help.

We've done target practice and lots of dry fire training and drills, but we've never fired our guns at living, breathing people. Our hand-to-hand combat training is pretty good, and Mom made sure we all know how to use a knife. But this . . . we aren't trained for a fight like this.

Chapter 15

Kimba

"You think that's good, Kimba?" Jameson points to the precariously leaning dead–fallen tree.

We're the last of the group in the woods along the river. As soon as we reached the cover of trees, Rey gave me an encouraging smile and said, "I'll be in contact." He and Atticus headed east along the path, in an area free of our concealed traps. The rest of us kept our eyes peeled, looking for fishing line to indicate a hazard.

One or two at a time, the others returned to the house. I swapped out the belly band holster and .22 revolver for my utility belt—my Glock and extra magazines now in their rightful place. The radio is clipped to my belt, waiting for the signal from Rey that they're in position. Then we'll head back.

Will the ruse work? There's no way to know for sure.

Well, there's one way: the watchers get antsy and call in the cavalry. If that happens, everything changes. It'll be a scramble for survival. Atticus assured Rey that, from their location hidden behind the watchers, they'll be able to see anyone coming up the road.

Once back at the house, the teens will have naps in preparation for tonight's mission, while the other women and I stay on watch. The traps along the river could come in handy, slowing our attackers and causing them to yell out, alerting us to their approach. We discussed taking a folding shovel and digging one of the pits, out of sight in the woods, but with the tree roots, holes don't make much sense.

This trap Jameson and I are finishing has the potential to be deadly. The combination of a trip wire and snare noose, along with the heavy fallen limb, could kill a man. Or it could just trap him—our desired intention. The likelihood of a fatality from this is low enough to make it worth the risk.

"I think it'll do."

"The bear horn was a great idea. I'm surprised my brother thought of it." Jameson motions several feet ahead of us where a trip wire of heavy fishing line is in place.

"It was brilliant. We had something similar at one of the summertime observation posts in Bakerville that was made from a boat horn. Him asking about it sparked Axel's memory of the bear horns they have. Setting it up so when the wire is tripped and a branch falls on it, making the horn blow, is perfect. We'll definitely hear it go off. Of course, they'll know we set it up for sure."

"Well, after the snare and spiderweb thing, then this log shooting at them, they can't be surprised, right?"

"Right."

He swats at a mosquito. "I've never even heard of a bear horn, and I've lived in bear country my entire life."

I wave a hand, brushing another one of the bloodsuckers away. "I didn't know about them either, but I guess they're a thing."

"Seems a little odd to be out hiking and blowing a horn every half mile to scare away wildlife." He scrunches up his face. "Although, maybe if we'd blown the horn, Jennifer— "

"No. That was different. The bear knew we were there. He targeted her—targeted their tent. He purposely went after them."

Jameson bobs his head. "My mom could've been killed too."

My eyes meet his. "Your mom was pretty amazing, the way she fought."

"She never fought my dad."

I tilt my head, waiting for him to say more. When he doesn't, I say, "I'm sure your mom did the best she could."

He lifts a shoulder. "He was always mean to her. No matter what she did, how hard she tried to make him happy, he'd snap at her. At all of us. Sometimes he'd be normal, like other dads, but then he'd go back to being super demanding. After the EMP, things got really bad. Then he turned abusive and started hitting us. But what could she do?" Jameson lifts his hands. "It's not like she could get a divorce in the middle of the apocalypse."

I drop my gaze. Indeed. Separating, divorcing . . . definitely not easy now. If we get rid of Brower and the threat we're under, I could return to my plan of sending Rey to Bozeman while the girls and I stay here.

My mouth goes dry. We've been so miserable. But the last few days, something seems to be shifting. Where he was aloof with me, he seems to be trying to draw us closer, to bring back what we had.

But I'm not ready. I hurt so much. So, so much. And I blame him—blame him for our son's death. I blame my husband almost as much as I blame myself.

"Uh, Kimba? You okay?"

I answer with a thin smile. "Let's disguise this a little better."

We spend several minutes working on our trap. We've just finished when the radio gives three short bursts: the signal Rey and Atticus are set and in position.

"Go back to the house now?" Jameson asks.

"Yup. Let's go through the trees here so we don't risk setting off any of the traps or alarms."

"Good idea. I'm having a hard time remembering where we put them all."

Back at the house, Axel and Victoria are on watch. Nicole and Brett are already in the basement, trying to rest. I send Axel and Jameson to join them.

Patti's main focus is her children and Naomi. They're in the living room while she watches out the window in the adjoining kitchen. We've closed the light-colored blinds, but she'll still ensure they stay away from the windows as they quietly play.

I wish Naomi could be my focus. We could just spend the day lounging around, reading books, and talking about everything and nothing. My baby's losing out on too much. *I'm* losing out on too much.

"Kimba?" Patti calls out in a soft voice from the kitchen. "I think you should see this."

"Victoria? You have eyes?"

"Um, yes. I'm watching them," she says from the second window in the office. I carefully move from the main window and stride to the kitchen. "What is it?"

"Watch." She points out the bay window. "Up on the hillside. I got a glimpse of—there! See it? I think it's a head."

I scan the area with my binoculars. It's several seconds before I see anything—the slight bob of something just a few inches above the horizon. While I can't be sure it's a head, I can't say it isn't.

"It could be them, trying to stay out of sight on their way to relieve the others," I say. "I'll let Victoria know. She'll take the main window in the office, and I'll move to where I've set up the diversion."

"Should we use Naomi as a messenger?"

My heart beats slightly out of tune as I glance toward my daughter.

She gives an energetic nod. "I'll be the messenger. Whatever Patti or Victoria tell me, I'll tell you."

"Remember to always stay low when you're near the windows so you don't make a shadow."

"There's no windows in the hallway. I can run like the wind when I get there."

I can't help but smile. "Run carefully."

Following my own advice, I stay low as I move through the living room. When I reach the hall, I straighten and turn back to my daughter, giving her a wink.

She winks in response.

At the door to the office, I inform Victoria I'm moving to the master bedroom patio to hide behind the AC unit, where Brett was stationed earlier.

She glances toward me. "They're here?"

"Maybe?" I briefly detail what we saw and how it may be them so we should get ready.

"Wish we had another radio so we could communicate between us. Should we wake the kids?"

"Not yet. If it's actually shift change for the watchers, the fireworks will wake them for us."

A smile flits across her face. "There've been plenty of times even fireworks wouldn't have woken my boys. I guess we all sleep a lot lighter these days."

"If you see anything definitive to indicate it's shift change, send Naomi out with the message. She's excited to help."

"Will do. Do you want me at the other window?"

"Please. Don't fire your gun unless I give the order or you hear me shooting, okay?"

She responds with a nod.

I pause a moment before asking, "And you're sure you can do it?"

Victoria's eyebrows raise in question. "Am I sure I can shoot a person?"

"Well . . . yes. Until the last few days, you haven't wanted anything to do with the guns."

"I still want nothing to do with them, but . . . it's different. I realized there's a need for them. They're a tool to protect us. I know how to shoot, and I'll do what I must. I appreciate you giving me the

.22. While I've never shot one so fancy, I'm familiar with the recoil and the noise they make. I don't think I'd feel as good shooting a cannon like you have."

I let out a laugh. "I've never really thought of a .308 as a cannon, but okay. Let's just hope you don't need to use yours and I don't need mine. Maybe . . ." I lift a hand.

"Yes, maybe. Maybe God will give us another one of those miracles. He's been good to us so far."

I bite my lip and shake my head. "Has He? Anyway, wait for my signal before doing anything."

I move down the hallway, through the bedroom, and into position outside. I set my rifle against the side of the house and my messenger bag next to it. I take a small disposable lighter—salvaged from a house during our travels—out of my pants pocket, testing the flame. It ignites immediately. I feel my lips drift upward in a smile.

Just to be sure, I unzip the outer bag of my pack and take out a plastic baggie containing several books of matches—more found items.

Two packs of Black Cat firecrackers were set out here earlier by one of the boys, ready for my use. The plan is to light one and throw it, aiming for a spot Atticus dug up to remove the grass. It's been a wet year, but fire danger is still a concern. So much so, there's a five-gallon bucket of water at the ready in case the grass sparks.

The noise of the firecrackers, along with the watchers trying to figure out what's happening, should be enough to allow Rey and Atticus to do what's needed . . . as long as the string isn't a dud. If it is, I'll try the second batch.

If neither set of firecrackers do what they're supposed to, then I'll get creative and do something outlandish or embarrassing to try and attract the watchers' full attention.

I hope the fireworks go off. I don't feel like putting on a show. I've had enough of pretending. Acting like a weak and incompetent fool around Lance Brower and Scott is too much. Like Nicole says, it's embarrassing.

I may be good at it, pretending to be someone I'm not, but my heart's no longer in it. When it was my job, what I was trained to do, that was one thing. But now . . . I'm done pretending.

As I wait, I focus on my breathing. It's important to stay in the moment and make sure I'm alert and mistake free.

It's only a few minutes until Naomi whispers from the door, "They definitely saw someone, and he may be in your view soon."

I thank her and remind her to be ready for a few loud bangs.

"Should I cover baby Trish's ears?"

"No need. It won't be too loud. Stay in the living room with them and you'll be fine."

"Okay, Mommy." The door closes with a soft click.

Catching movement near the watchers, my heart accelerates. I stay low as I watch two men slide in through the brush next to the others. They briefly chat and then one raises his binoculars.

I shrink down and out of sight. I work on my calming breaths and flick the lighter again. It flares up as it should. Now it's a waiting game for the radio to click. After that, more waiting.

We won't really know when they're far enough away to not hear the fireworks, to not be alerted something is wrong, which could cause them to either return to the watch location or call for help.

The single click of the walkie-talkie sounds, indicating the relief group has taken over and the originals are leaving. The click also means Rey and Atticus are still hidden and safe.

My marriage may be floundering, but the worry of my husband being injured—or worse—is high. While separating sounds like it may be an easy solution, a way to help heal my broken heart, I know it's not.

Even if we were still living happily in Denver, if things were normal, it wouldn't be easy to be apart. I want what we used to have. The closeness we enjoyed. The companionship. The friendship.

Rey and I were friends before we were lovers. We met under difficult circumstances. He went out of his way to be kind to me, to help me through my troubles. Our friendship went on for months. Then, one day, I realized it was more. It was love.

I carefully rise up, just enough to see the watchers' hideout. The two replacements are older and rougher looking than the previous pair. They also seem to be paying little attention to us. One is leaning back with his eyes closed. The other is reading a book.

I almost laugh out loud at their version of keeping watch. Of course, earlier we had Nicole on the porch with a book.

My stomach clenches. The book was for Scott's benefit, to make it seem like she was just relaxing. He didn't fall for it. Did he report back to Brower? Did Scott tell them we know we're being watched? Is his book a hint?

I swallow hard, realizing the implications. All we've planned could be useless. These two could be a plant, a diversion while the attackers are getting into position.

I close my eyes and strain my ears, listening for any of the noisemakers. They'd either come up the river or from over the hill, behind the watchers. Those are the only two locations they could approach without being seen. In the dark, they could come from any direction, but not now. Not during the daylight.

What do we do? Go with the original plan? Change things? I shake my head. I can't make any changes without alerting Rey over the radio. I can't alert him without risking the watchers hearing. We stick with this, see it through.

"Mom?" Naomi hisses from the patio door. "Patti says she thinks the two are gone. She said maybe five more minutes."

"Okay. I need you to wake up Jameson. We need another sentry."

"I can be a sentry."

My heart swells with pride. "I know you can. But I need you to keep up your job as messenger. Bring Jameson to the patio door. Quick, before the five minutes are up."

Much quicker than I expect, Jameson's at the door, asking where I want him.

I send him to the front porch, out of sight of the watchers but able to see a good expanse of the trees along the river and the property line fence. I don't share my concerns with him, but he must know something is up from the tension in my voice. "Let them know I'm setting off the firecrackers in two minutes."

Two minutes later, I take a deep breath. With the string of firecrackers in one hand and the lighter in the other, I mutter, "Please, God, if you're still listening to me, let this work."

A smile plays at my lips when the fuse ignites. I lob it out to the dirt patch. Within seconds, I'm rewarded with a satisfying *pop, pop, pop.* I light and toss the second string, internally rejoicing when it also goes off. I hope it was enough for Rey and Atticus to do what was needed.

My stomach is sour, and I'm shaking. After taking a minute to compose myself, I lift up my binoculars. I'm rewarded with the sight of my husband pulling the book reader behind the shrubs. Atticus has the napper. With tears stinging my eyes, I wait until Rey returns to my view.

He searches me out and raises his hand before signaling they're on their way back. As planned, they'll return the same way they left, just in case someone else is watching that we haven't located.

The rattle of cans causes me to jump. One of the noisemakers. Way too close.

Chapter 16

Kimba

I flip around and grab my rifle. I catch a streak of gray cresting the hill a hundred yards away, running at what must be near the speed of light.

My mind registers it's a deer, not a threat, but my body reacts differently. My breath comes in short gasps. The world begins to tilt as my hands go numb. A crushing feeling starts in the middle of my chest. I let out a low moan and close my eyes.

Breathe. Slow. Count them. Breathe.

"Mommy?"

Exhale. One, two, three, four . . .

"Mommy? Are you okay? Mommy?"

Inhale. One, two, three, four . . .

"Mommy! Mommy!"

"Kimba? Kimba, what's wrong?"

Hold the breath . . .

Breathing out through my nose, I crack open an eye.

Patti is on her knee. She grabs my tingling hand and gives it a squeeze. "You're okay. Breathe out through your mouth. Good, good. Now in through your nose."

She talks me through another round of breathing.

"Better?" she asks with a hint of a smile.

I shake my head. "It happened again. What're we going to do if— "

"Hey, you're okay. *We're* going to be okay."

I close my eyes and give a weary sway of my head. "We shouldn't be here."

"Enough." Patti's voice turns steely. Harsh. "We are here, and we will do this. The plan is solid."

"The plan is stupid. We should— "

"We can't. Not without trying."

"You're willing to risk your children's lives?"

"I'm not. If things go bad, we'll get out. I'll make sure not only my children but also Naomi are safe. I give you my word. I will protect Naomi, take her to Simms— "

"And Nicole?"

Her mouth becomes a tight, colorless line. "You know Rey will do what he can. Atticus too. They will— "

I lift a hand. "There're no guarantees."

She drops her shoulders and lets out a breath. "There aren't. Not in anything. Even before all this, there weren't any guarantees."

I put my hand to my forehead as tears sting my eyes. "I didn't used to be like this. I never had trouble keeping it together. The jobs . . ." I lift a shoulder. "I don't know what's wrong with me."

"Grief. Did you . . . have you told Rey? When it happened the first time— "

I wave her away with my hand. "He doesn't need to know. It's always afterward, never in the middle."

She raises her eyebrows as her eyes meet mine. The first time this happened—a panic attack—was when we were hiding out after a middle-of-the-night shooting. We weren't being shot at; the gunfire was in a town nearby.

Just before dawn, Rey and Atticus went to find out what happened. They'd only been gone a few minutes when the tightening in my chest started and my hands went numb. Everyone else, except Patti, was asleep. Like today, she helped me breathe through it.

At the time, I thought it was a heart attack. I'd never had anything like that happen before. No way. I never would've been able to be an operations officer or done the consulting work with Rey. Being levelheaded and always in control of my emotions was imperative.

Now look at me. I'm a blubbering mess.

I shake my head again. "He doesn't need to know."

"How many times? Other than today and the first time? When the bear attacked?"

"No . . . almost. But it went away. It's never been as bad as the first time. Not until today."

"And the breathing, you call it box breathing, huh? It helps?"

I tilt my head. "It's fine. I'm fine now."

"Before, back when you were . . . when you relied on staying calm— "

"You mean when I was a spy?" I make my eyes go wide.

She responds with a nervous laugh. "Yeah. You learned the box breathing then, right?"

"Why?"

"I was thinking, maybe your specific pattern might be a . . ." She crinkles her nose. "Maybe it's a trigger of sorts. Instead of calming you like it should, it takes you back to those days."

I wave her away. "I'm fine. Let's get inside and get ready for what's next. Did the firecrackers wake everyone up?"

She bites her top lip and then opens her mouth, but then abruptly closes it and shakes her head. "Not sure. As far as I know, the teens are all still sleeping."

I shake my head and give a slight smile. "Proof they can sleep through anything."

Inside the house, Victoria has all the younger children in the living room.

Naomi sees me in the hallway and gives me a slight wave. "Are you okay now, Mommy? Did you see a bee?"

I can't help but chuckle. My daughter has an aversion to things that fly and can sting. I've seen her completely lose it over a wasp before. "Something like that. I'm okay now."

"What happened?" Nicole asks as she steps out of the kitchen with a mug in her hand. Peppermint tea. I can smell it.

"I didn't realize you were up."

She gives me a look I interpret as *duh*. "You set off fireworks. I thought you'd give us a warning. I bolted out of bed and slammed into Brett in the hallway."

I shake my head. "I wasn't thinking. I wanted to let you sleep as long as possible so you're ready for . . . for . . ."

"For later? Well, I'm up now."

"Brett? Axel?"

"They went back to bed. Where's Dad? Did everything go okay?"

"I think so, yes. They should be back anytime."

"You want some tea? This is stuff we brought. No bugs in it. There's still a little water. Axel checked the propane tank earlier. It's nearly full, so we can easily cook on the stovetop. I sure wish the hot water heater still worked. I'd love a shower."

I stare at my eldest daughter, wondering how she can talk about such trivial things. Her dad and Atticus just killed two men. She may need to do the same thing later. She may need to kill. And here she is talking about food and showers.

I purse my lips. I was like that once—able to compartmentalize, shift from normal life to doing what was needed and then back again.

It was always easy. Too easy maybe. I was confident in my skills, arrogant even. That's what caused the troubles, what changed my life and had me finding a new line of work.

And now look at me.

No way could I ever go back to it. I straighten my shoulders. I may not ever be an operator again, but I'm going to get myself together and do what's needed to defeat Brower. I'll make sure Axel and Atticus, along with the Dawsons and Patti and her children, are safe. This will be a good place for them. With so many supplies and things still available, they'll be comfortable for months ahead.

I can do it. I can get my head back in the game and do what's needed.

Nicole furrows her brow. "What?"

As my heart swells with love, I motion with my hand. "I'd love some tea."

"There's cornmeal mush," Patti says, "from the opened bag of masa in the cabinet. I uh, I checked it. It was clear."

Nicole makes a face. "Just because you didn't *see* any bugs, doesn't mean they weren't in there walking around. Gross."

Patti lifts a shoulder. "I found honey to drizzle over it, and coconut oil. If you melt the oil in a little water, it makes a creamy milk-like substance. LJ loved the mush I made for him."

My stomach gives a rumble at the thought of food, even if it might've had pests walking through it. Other than some deer jerky, I've eaten little today. With Victoria on watch in the office and Jameson at the front, I make myself a bowl and sit so I can look out the kitchen window—a good view of the property line dividing the Double D and Brower's ranch, along with the paved road leading west toward Augusta, Montana.

I may prefer we not fight, convince the Dosen boys to move to Simms, but what Brower's doing is wrong. His desire to eliminate the other ranches, to take over all the land by force, is reprehensible. The worst part of it is he sits in his mansion—his ivory tower—and commands others to do his dirty work.

A slight smile plays at my lips as I recall Rey getting the man worked up. If he had it in him, if Brower had any guts at all, he'd lead the charge to eliminate Rey, to put him in his place. But men like Brower may get a little alcohol in them and talk big, but ultimately, it's unsustainable.

My guess is, even in his previous life, his business life, he had a whole group of employees and contractors he could call on for anything that needed doing. I've known plenty of men like him. Worked for them even. In our business, Rey and I marketed ourselves as problem solvers. While it's true, we solved problems, many times it was with a gun, and too often it was for people like Brower.

We tried to be picky, to only work for those who had a cause we believed in, but it doesn't change much. It doesn't change the fact we were hired killers and sometimes on the wrong side of things. How many innocents are dead because of us? Because my research didn't divulge the truth of what was actually happening?

I run a finger along my forearm, tracing the scarred, jagged line: a reminder of a time that went bad. It definitely wasn't an innocent then—the woman was like me, a trained killer. The scar on my arm is nothing compared to the one on my back, also complements of her.

There're others, too, a dimple in my leg from a small caliber bullet—just a graze, but it sure did sting. The physical scars, easily covered and mostly out of sight, are still reminders of the past.

After the EMP and ending up in Bakerville, my past slapped me in the face when Doris Snyder—who I previously knew as Meagan Wright—held me at gunpoint. She could've killed me, would've if she'd followed her training, but she didn't. I saw the doubt as her eyes flicked from me to Rey and then to our children.

Instead of an instant death, Rey and I were taken hostage, separated from our kids. Eventually, I found out the weakness I thought I'd seen in Doris was strength. Sometime in the years since she'd left government service, she'd found God.

At first, I got a good laugh out of it. Doris, when living as Meagan, had done the same rotten things as me. She'd been an operations officer for years before, a true chameleon. She'd aged out of much of the field work and was working as a handler. *My* handler.

To say it was a rocky relationship would be an understatement. I was well trained but green. She was well trained and seasoned. And she hated me from the minute we met.

Our employer—an offshoot of a well-known government agency—started us off small, sending us on easy missions. I proved myself over and over, or so I thought. Meagan rarely gave me a kind word or accolade. She'd occasionally grunt a begrudging *good job*, but then she'd launch into a detailed diatribe of what I'd done wrong.

Her hatred for me in those early days of Bakerville were no surprise. Meagan blamed me for the death of her fiancé.

She insisted I was a double agent and I'd intentionally caused his death. She'd made such a stink during the investigation, I really had no choice but to quit. That wasn't enough for her; she wanted me prosecuted, tried for treason. Sentenced to death.

It was Rey, employed by a different country but in the same line of work, whose testimony eventually cleared me. Our relationship was what forced him out. Even though I was cleared, the accusations were a blight on me and Rey loving me meant he couldn't be trusted.

Meagan, known as Doris in Bakerville, which she insists is her real name, eventually forgave me. At first, it was just like the *good jobs* she'd begrudgingly give—I don't think she really meant it. She was offering me forgiveness because she said forgiving me was the right thing to do. *The Christian thing.*

Eventually it was more. She not only forgave me, but we reconciled. We became true friends. She became a grandma to the children. My heart hurts thinking how much she, too, would be grieving if she knew of Nate's death.

"There's Rey and Atticus," Patti says. "They're almost to the front door."

I take my empty bowl to the sink, then move to the living room to meet the men.

Once inside, Rey flashes me a brief smile. "It went as expected. Mostly."

I raise my eyebrows. "Mostly?"

He runs a hand through his hair. "Scott was right about the walkie-talkies. And the ones they were relieving made a point of saying to remember to check in."

I let out a noisy breath. "And if they don't?"

"They'll send the crew."

Chapter 17

Kimba

"They'll send the rest of their gang?" Nicole's voice is full of alarm. "What are we going to do?"

Atticus gives her a sly smile. "Pretend to be them. We heard it all. The guys leaving—Fedler and . . ." He looks to Rey.

"Doesn't matter." Rey gives a wave of his hand. "What matters is they told the new guys when to check in and what to say, and to be sure to enunciate because the transmission is terrible."

I raise my eyebrows. "That seems . . ."

"Suspicious?" Rey's mustache twitches. "No doubt. My entire body tensed when I heard it, thought for sure it was some sort of set up. But they left and the, uh, the rest— " his eyes meet mine as he raises his eyebrows slightly " —went off without incident."

My shoulders drop. The casual way we're discussing the death of two men is hard to stomach. It had to happen, and more will happen before this is over, but still.

Even as someone trained to compartmentalize, to do what's needed for self and country, the killing has always troubled me. Not excessively, and not to the point I couldn't cope, but it's always there. I remember all of them. Sometimes, doing what's necessary can leave scars. And not just physical ones.

"When's check in?"

"Every three hours. They were even kind enough to leave a watch." He motions to Atticus's wrist.

When we left the ski lodge, we had a watch too. It broke along the way. At first, I hated not knowing what time it was, but soon we got used to looking at the sky and estimating.

Not that time really matters. Walking every day, we'd use the mile markers along the highway to gauge our distance. We had daily goals and strived to meet them, but for the most part, we'd stop when we were tired and eat when we were hungry. We go to bed with the sun and get up with it. We're like so many people throughout history who lived by the natural rhythms of the sun.

"Did they say anything about attacking us?"

"Quite a lot, in fact. The replacements were here for the duration— " He clears his throat. "That was the plan anyway. They told the guys leaving they'd been instructed to take turns napping and to make sure they were ready at dawn to pick off any of us who came running out."

"Running out? They plan to burn the house?"

"That's the way I took it."

My mouth goes tight. "Just this place, or the big house too?"

Rey shakes his head. "No details."

Atticus crosses his arms. "I don't want them burning down *either* of my houses."

"What about all the supplies?" Nicole asks. "There's a lot of stuff in this place."

Atticus rubs his scruffy chin. "In our house too. When I went in with Scott earlier, I couldn't believe it. All the things we had are still there, a mess like Scott said. Mountains of our stuff in messy piles. And there's more. In another section there's boxes of food and supplies, all neatly organized. It looks like a warehouse. I hate to think where it came from. Scott ignored it and didn't say anything about it, and I didn't ask. I wanted to, but I didn't."

Rey clucks his tongue. "Doesn't make much sense, them being willing to burn us out when there're things they need here."

"Maybe that's not the plan," I say. "Maybe they're just planning to invade. They think we're weak, so they'll come in while they think we're sleeping and overrun us. Just like— " My voice cracks.

"Just like Bakerville proper—the river people," Atticus says. "The way they were attacked, Richard Majors's people simply went in and slaughtered them while they slept."

There are several moments of silence as we each remember the massacre that left all but five children dead. Murdered.

"Nope. No way we'll let it happen," Axel says from the hallway. His hair is mussed from sleep, but his jaw is firm. "We're going to end this. We're going to stop Brower and his terrorizing."

"That's the plan." Atticus's crisp blue eyes meet his brother's identical ones. "Then we can start rebuilding and truly helping the surrounding towns, not just keeping them supplied with liquor."

We move to the kitchen so anyone hungry can eat. Brett, groggy from sleep, soon joins us. While they're eating, Rey asks Atticus what other useful things he saw in the house. The fireworks were definitely a great find. Since we're no longer being watched, we plan to weaponize them, turning them into improvised explosive devices—IEDs.

Rey slides his chair from the table. "We'd best get a move on. I want to be in position, watching Brower's place, so we can see them leave."

"When do you think that'll be?" Atticus asks.

"They'll be antsy, excited," I say. "Especially the ones who enjoy this."

Atticus makes a face. "I don't know how they can enjoy killing."

"They'll want to be in place at least an hour before daylight."

"Two probably," Rey corrects. "Like you said, they'll be antsy. They'll push it, wanting to attack while it's still mostly dark."

I lean back in my chair. "We should move to the fort shortly after sunset. You're sure the escape is acceptable? If it's obvious we're going to be overrun, Patti will be able to get the children out?"

Rey gestures with his hand while nodding. "It's good. While we start working on things, why don't you go set it up? Get a good view in the daylight and make your plans."

"I'll take Victoria with me, unless you need her here?"

"I'd like to go too," Patti says. "I was thinking a cache might be a good idea, somewhere on the way to Simms."

"What'd you have in mind?"

"Maybe the wagon? We could put a few essentials in it and hide it in the brush."

"Let's do it," Rey says. "We'd better get going. It's going to be time to check in with Brower's men soon."

My stomach clenches at all the things we need to do in such a short amount of time. Rey puts Axel and Brett on watch while he, Atticus, Nicole, and Jameson make the IEDs. Naomi and the babies are in the basement, while Victoria, Patti, and I head to the hideout.

Chapter 18

Nicole

"How's this different than the booby traps along the river?" Jameson asks as we put a bunch of nails in an old soup can.

My dad's mouth goes into a tight line. "We'll have them in places they'll most likely use to come after those of you in the hideout fort— in the trees along the ridge, plus the game trail heading straight up. Likely, they'll take the ridgeline, but you never know."

"Are these . . ." Jameson tilts his head to one side.

"Fatal?"

"Yeah."

"In today's world, probably."

"When did you learn how to make these?"

With raised eyebrows, my dad gives Jameson a meaningful look.

The blush starts at Jameson's neck. "I mean . . . I guess you'd know how in your line of work."

"Everything we're putting together—the noisemakers, the traps, the IEDs—were all available via a quick internet search."

"Humph," Jameson snorts. "Great way to have the NSA show up on your doorstep."

I let out a laugh. Jameson sounds just like Donnie McCullough. Donnie was a huge conspiracy theorist, convinced everything happening to us now was a plot by either our own government or a rogue group known as the Deep State. Donnie was quite a character.

The scary thing is, my mom and dad didn't outright disagree with him on any of it. They didn't agree either, but they also didn't say he was wrong. I suspect they have their own theories about who's responsible for the terrorist attacks and the nuclear strikes. I've asked, but they change the subject and give me zero information. Sometimes they forget I'm no longer a child.

Thinking of Donnie makes me wonder how Sadie's doing. Out of everyone in our group, Sadie was the biggest surprise. When we left the ski lodge, I thought she was a frightened little kid, scared of her own shadow. Turns out she was a lot tougher, and older, than I knew.

When traveling through Great Falls, we heard rumors of mail service starting up. I've decided I'm going to write a letter to Sadie. I'm not really sure how that'll work out since we're not settling in one place yet, but I can at least let Sadie and her family know about Nate and Jennifer. We were all so close, like family, and they need to know.

I've never actually written a letter before. I've sent a ton of texts and instant messages, plus a fair number of emails. I've signed my name and written short greetings on birthday cards, of course. Letter writing is not—or *was* not—a thing when we had the internet and phones.

Now, with those things gone, we're back to the old days. Even the mail service will be like something out of the past, traveling on horseback like the Pony Express and utilizing the transports starting up on the interstates and major highways.

We spend many minutes working in silence, until Atticus makes a noise that causes me to look in his direction.

His eyes are moist as he shakes his head. "The guys who were watching us, not the first pair but the two that we . . ." His voice fades away, and he clears his throat. "We did them a favor by killing them quick. The way they were talking . . . a slow, agonizing death is what they deserved."

I stop what I'm doing and look fully at him. "Meaning?"

My dad makes a motion with his hand. "It's not important to know the details."

Atticus shakes his head. "They were not good guys. The ones who left sounded okay, good friends who'd known each other awhile. I don't think they wanted to be here. Rey?"

"Sounded like it."

"Yeah, they didn't agree with watching us, said so several times while we were hiding out behind them. They thought it was stupid. Then they talked about some of the other things that happened to the families Brower attacked. I don't think they were involved, not directly. They've always had the role of sentry. One of them even said he'd tried to render first aid, but someone else shot the injured man right between the eyes and said Brower didn't want any hostages."

I look to my dad, who's studiously avoiding my gaze. It's hard to think of him as a killer, to know he and Atticus just took two lives. While Atticus is clearly shaken up about it, Dad seems okay. Before the world fell apart, I never thought he and Mom weren't exactly what they seemed: excellent and loving parents and the owners of a consulting business.

He's so mild mannered, so normal. And he's always been a great dad. Mom was always great too. Well, mostly. Sometimes she'd drive me crazy with her momness. But I guess it was to be expected. We'd butt heads on occasions, but she was still pretty great. I know she wanted the best for me, for all of us.

Now, with the trouble between them, I'm not sure how things will work out. But I know what I'm doing. I'm going to stop Brower. Then, if my mom wimps out and says she's staying here, I'm gone. I've got my own salvaged jewelry and other trinkets I can use for trade.

Jameson lets out a loud sigh. "Why would Brower do this? What about— " His voice cracks.

Dad rests a hand on Jameson's back. "There's evil in the world."

Atticus scoffs. "No kidding. The two who replaced them, the ones we . . . they were evil. They sounded almost excited about their role in our attack. They were supposed to pick off any survivors trying to get away. But that's not what they wanted to do, not by a long shot. The things they said . . . it was right to kill them."

My dad puts a hand on Atticus's shoulder. "It had to be done. Sometimes, the things we must do aren't pleasant. They're terrible, in fact. But in order to protect our family, we do what we must."

"What about the two that left?" Jameson asks. "Will they be a part of attacking us?"

Dad and Atticus look at each other. Dad shakes his head. "Don't know. From what we heard, it didn't sound like they know much about the attack. The other two didn't either, other than their role, which we know won't happen now."

I meet my dad's eyes. "You're sure this is the right thing to do?"

"It has to happen," Atticus says quickly. "We can't let Brower have our ranch. We can't let him keep doing what he's doing—stealing, killing people. It's not right."

"It isn't right." Dad agrees with a nod. "Truthfully, I'd rather send your mom and the others away. You too. Send everyone back to Simms and take care of this on my own."

"Not me." Atticus shakes his head. "I'm not expecting you to fight my fight—not alone."

"I know. And your brother, no way would he let this rest. We'll do what we must. I think, if we get rid of Lance Brower, it'll stop. If the two we overheard are any indication, there're plenty of others who don't believe in what they're doing. They thought they were taking jobs as ranch hands in exchange for food and lodging. They didn't sign up for the killing."

"But the other two— " I motion to the hillside across the road, where their bodies are stashed in the brush. "You said they were okay with it."

"I should've asked Connor," Atticus says. "When he was here earlier, we could've got information from him about the men his dad has."

"We couldn't risk him suspecting we might fight back."

"Don't you think Brower knew?" I ask. "Besides, Connor isn't like his dad, right? The things he said . . ."

"He hates his dad," Atticus blurts. "Always has."

Dad gives a weak smile. "Still, family is family. Connor may not like the things his dad does, may not even like him as a person. But when it comes down to it, he's still his dad."

I drop my gaze back to my work. I finish filling the can to the amount my dad said and pass it on to Jameson, who'll duct tape the top.

Dad's right about family. Last year, when I found out about my mom and dad, it changed a lot—changed the way I felt about them, especially my mom. I watched her kill a man with her bare hands. Snapped his neck like it was a twig. She did it to save me after two men kidnapped me and planned to . . . I squeeze my eyes tight. I hate to think about what their plans for me were.

Up until then, I thought my mom and dad were marketing consultants. I knew they had a few peculiarities. My dad, who lived in England until he married my mom, would often fake an American accent. After so many years of being in the US, his British was mild. But sometimes, he'd make it go away completely, usually when we went on vacation or were in situations where we'd never see the people again.

And Mom would sometimes act really weird too. Normally, she was extremely confident and capable. But in certain circumstances, she'd act like a dumb blond or an incompetent twit—or worse, a huge flirt.

The first time I realized she was doing it, I wasn't much older than Naomi is now. We were in a store, looking at a new dining room table. We'd just moved to Denver and bought the condo. The salesman was the slimy kind who talked down to my mom. She batted her eyelashes a few times and acted like she didn't have a clue what she was looking for.

The man puffed up his chest and started spouting off all kinds of stuff about tables, like they were some kind of special works of art. It was very odd. We didn't buy a table, and I don't remember ever going back to that store.

When I asked my mom about it later, why she suddenly seemed to change, she waved me off, saying she'd explain when I was older. Eventually, I realized it was a way for her to manipulate people, to get what she wanted. Now I know it's more. She reads people and situations and adapts. It was annoying and odd when the world was normal, but now it helps keep us alive.

I suck in my top lip. Since Nate died, she's lost her edge. When Brower was here and she was putting on her show, it seemed so fake. He seemed to fall for it, but I don't think Scott did. Just like he didn't think I was really sitting on the porch reading a book. He knew my job was lookout. Having the rifle nearby might have been part of the clue, but everyone has guns now, so . . .

No, there's something about Scott. I don't think we're fooling him much, if at all. Atticus was smart to set up the noisemakers with him, but we'd probably be even smarter to move them to different locations. We don't know where the man's loyalties lie—with the brothers he's known for years, or with the dad of his fiancée?

They're certainly an odd couple. Tara Brower is only a few years older than me. Scott is probably in his thirties. He's handsome enough, but it seems someone like Tara, someone obviously used to the finer things in life, would want more than a ranch hand.

Maybe, like Connor said, she's just using Scott until someone better comes along and she has no intention of marrying him. Does it even matter? Right now, today, Scott seems committed to her. Committed enough he's gone to the Brower mansion for the night. He knows Brower plans to attack us, and instead of being willing to stay and fight, he left.

Without looking up, I ask, "You're sure we're doing the right thing?"

I feel my dad stiffen. "I think it's a solid plan, Nic. But I also know your mom has a point. Leaving the ranch and letting the courts sort it out later would be the safer choice."

"But . . . but," Atticus stutters, "I thought you said— "

My dad lifts a hand. "I do believe Brower will continue his murderous rampage. Soon, he won't be satisfied just wiping out ranches and killing families. He'll try and take Simms or another small town. He'll band with another gang maybe. Brower is trouble, that much is obvious. He needs to be stopped. And we'll do it."

Chapter 19

Kimba

The hideout is everything Rey promised. The boulders, which are visible from the house, are even larger in person. Plenty big enough to provide adequate cover and concealment.

The depression in the earth is deep, then opens at the back where it's lined with a few scraggly trees. Atticus said the water collects here during the wet season, resulting in a shallow pond and adding just enough moisture to sustain the sparse woodlands.

I'll admit, I never thought much about rain and trees and such until after the collapse. Sure, I knew the basics and could appreciate a beautiful park or forest. But I never even thought about how the trees grow thicker along bodies of water.

And I never realized the importance of snow and rain. We had what many referred to as record snowfall last winter—even for an area used to receiving an abundance.

Like the snowfall, the spring had record rain. Many, like Atticus and his family, said the wet spring was good. It'd help give the cattle plenty of grass not only for the summer months but to harvest and stack, carrying them through winter.

Atticus was right. The Double D has an abundance of grass. He's even begrudgingly admitted the cattle have been rotated well and Scott and Brower's crew have done a fine job with haying, resulting in several old-time stacks.

Last year, in the late summer and fall, we lived in Bakerville. When we weren't on militia duty, we took shifts working the fields. Haying, harvesting sugar beets, cutting corn stalks, digging potatoes . . . all hard and backbreaking work but necessary to survive the winter.

"You think this will work?" Victoria asks, jolting me from my thoughts. "We'll be able to keep an eye on them from here?"

I bob my head several times. "Easily. It's perfect."

"We should make another string of noisemakers to put at the back." Patti points to the wide opening, with a boulder on one side and a short, pathetic-looking tree on the other. "Maybe two even, one from each direction?"

"Good idea," I agree. "But I want to leave the path out clear. If we have to go, it may be in a hurry. We don't want to be tripping and falling." I put a finger to my chin. "But I do think . . ."

"Maybe one of those explosives Rey's making?" Patti raises her eyebrows. "We could set it up on our way out."

"I like the way you think. What do you need in place to make LJ and Trish more comfortable?"

"One of the sleeping pads. My hope is we can put them down and they'll zonk out. I still want to find a place to put our stuff. The spot where Nicole, Jameson, and I waited with the children might be good."

Nibbling on my lip, I think back to where we left them yesterday evening. *Yesterday evening?* Was it only twenty-four hours ago when we arrived here? So much has happened today—burying Jennifer, meeting Brower, going to his spacious ranch, discovering we were being watched. It feels like much longer than a day.

"That's too close. But let's get the things we need, and we'll find a spot."

Back at the house, the three of us pack up one of the large backpacks with several days' worth of necessities for LJ, Trish, and Naomi. Naomi will also have the pack she's carried for the last several hundred miles as we've walked across Montana.

LJ also has a small backpack with a thin blanket, a bag of jerky, a bottle of water, and a few other things—emergency items in case he was to somehow become separated from his mom or our group. Of course, at his young age of three, the few things in his pack won't help much without knowledge.

As we've traveled with Patti and her children, I've noticed she's been educating him along the way. She teaches as she does things, involving him in the day-to-day necessities of life in our off-the-grid world. He helps set up the tents, helps gather and purify water, helps make jerky and simple meals, all of it.

In the evenings, they'll look at the few books she has in her pack, books she brought with her on different survival aspects, even showing him the photos in the handwritten foraging book given to her by the wildcrafter from Mosher's community. Survival education needs to start early in today's world.

Naomi has also learned a lot about living in a world without electricity or much safety. Her training began when we lived in Bakerville and has continued on the road.

Nate was a big part of training his baby sister. He had a passion for all things wilderness and wanted her to learn. After Nate's death, the training dropped off. I need to talk to Rey, make a point to restart her education. She needs these survival skills.

Jameson started using Nate's slingshot to harvest food and has also tried to take over some of Naomi's training. But he doesn't have the knowledge or skills. When we lived in Bakerville, he didn't have the desire to learn. The first months we were on the road, he was sullen and testy, not at all interested in our journey or developing survival skills. He only started to come around, his nastiness easing to where he wasn't such a pain, when Nate was killed.

After Nate's death, Jameson transformed. He stepped up and tried to find his place not only in our group but in the world. A few days ago, he made the biggest change when he accepted Jesus as his Lord and Savior. I'm happy for him. Truly, I am. But I'm also well aware it's not the end all he currently believes.

Both he and Victoria prayed for salvation on that same night. Both are still floating on a cloud—the cloud of acceptance and a new passion. Even when Jennifer was attacked by the bear only a few hours later, I saw the comfort the Dawsons have in their new beliefs.

Atticus and Axel too. Even though they're hurting and angry after losing their mom, they know she's in Heaven with their dad and brother.

I wish I was like that.

I wish I could find the comfort in knowing my son is with Jesus. My brain may believe he is, even my heart, but I still hurt so much. I know I'm supposed to be happy for him, happy he's left the pain of this world and is now rejoicing.

But I want him back. I want him with me. I want to hear his laughter and feel his arms hugging me, even get a little of the teenage sass he was getting so good at. I wouldn't even mind seeing a roll of his eyes.

Does this pain ever go away? Will the hurt of losing him ever lessen?

"Kimba?" Patti taps me on the arm. "What do you think? Is it safe?"

I blink my eyes several times. "Um . . . sorry?"

She gives me a wan smile. "The children—can we bring them with us this time? I thought it might be good for Naomi and LJ to see the hideout in the daylight, see where we're leaving our stash."

"Oh! Yes, very smart."

"And you think it's safe for them to leave the house?"

I tilt my head to the side. "I don't think anyone else is watching us. If they are . . ." I lift a hand. "I don't think they are. And you're right about it being a good idea. They can get their bearings during the daylight."

Within a few minutes, the six of us are out the door. Trish is tied to Patti's chest in a fabric sling. LJ is walking, and I have a second carrier for him that we'll leave in the hideout or in the cache.

We decided against the wagon and are just bringing backpacks, smaller ones with essentials to keep with us in the hideout and the larger one to put in the cache with several days' worth of survival items.

Once in the hideout, I tell Naomi to look around and search for landmarks. She and LJ point out the houses and the river.

"It'll be dark when we come back here," I say. "It's good to get an idea while we're here of what things look like. Behind us, to the east, is the town of Simms. If we need to bug out, that's the direction we'll go. While we're in here, hiding, everyone needs to be very quiet. We can't risk the men hearing us."

LJ scrunches up his face. "Wha' if sisser cries?"

"I'm hoping she'll sleep," his mom answers. "And you too. We'll make a nice bed for you."

"In th' tent?"

"Under the stars."

His eyes go wide. "I like stars. We sing th'twinkle song?"

"Maybe while you're falling asleep. But remember, we'll be very quiet."

"I know how be quiet. LJ good at quiet. Push mouth together." He makes his mouth a tight line, which causes Naomi to laugh.

"You're funny, LJ." She turns to me. "How will we know if we need to leave?"

"One of us— " I motion to Victoria, Patti, and myself " —or Jameson will tell you. Now let's go find a place to put our extra stuff."

We exit through the back of the fort. Once we're out, Patti and I take a few moments to connect the noisemakers in likely paths toward the hideout, from both the direction of the Sun River and the paved road.

We survey the area heading east. It's fairly flat for twenty feet or so before beginning a gentle decline. Scruffy trees continue, with larger trees closer to the river, which takes a gentle curve toward the road at the bottom of the hill.

I can see why Atticus's ancestors chose this land. The area is truly breathtaking. The beauty of the river and the Rocky Mountains to the west, it's picturesque. A person would never tire of the views.

"Go to the road?" Patti asks.

I scan the area around the road. The trees end about fifty feet from it, and the other side is once again open, with the occasional jagged rock outcropping.

Since we left the ski lodge nearly six months ago, we've been in the high prairie or high desert—depending on who you ask. The wide-open spaces make for easy travel but terrible cover.

The trees will provide some concealment, but we'd be in full view if we moved to the other side of the road. I do like the looks of the hilltop—good cover because of the rocks and high ground. I like high ground.

Patti reaches for my left hand. "Let's pray. I think we should pray."

"Huh?"

"She's right," Victoria says. "I feel . . . we need to pray."

I stifle a sigh. "Fine. If you want."

"I want to, too, Mommy." Naomi reaches for my right hand as we gather in a circle.

Patti clears her throat. "Father God, here we are again, in . . . in a pickle. I know You're with us, guiding us and helping as we make our plans. While we've found this hideout, we know You are our true hiding place. It's under Your wings we can always find refuge, protection from the evil we may encounter.

"Please, God, keep us safe. Keep the rest of our family safe as they do what's necessary. None of us want this. We'd all be happy to live in peace, to avoid this fight and settle in. That doesn't seem to be the plan at the moment. But if You could, please step in and soften Lance Brower's heart and help him realize there's a way for all of us to coexist, that more violence and death isn't needed. You are our Protector. We trust in You."

Patti squeezes my hand, indicating she's finished and asking if I want to say something.

I give a slight shake of my head.

After a couple moments of silence, Victoria begins, "Um, God, praying isn't something I've done much of. Learning to talk with You isn't easy. I pray You can hear my heart and not my jumbled words. I'm scared. I'm not trained like Kimba and Rey, like Atticus or any of the boys. I'm afraid for Brett and Jameson, for all of us. I love these people.

"The Bible tells us You care for us and have a plan for us. If we believe in and receive Your Son, Jesus Christ, we become one of Your children. I know how much I love my children, how much each of us does. I can only imagine Your love for us is the same. You want to keep us from harm. Like Patti said, if You could stop this, we'd sure appreciate it."

I briefly consider saying something. But the truth is, I have zero confidence God will step in and stop this. Do I think He could? Sure. *He's God.* But will He? Doubtful. He didn't step in and save my son.

Patti waits a couple of seconds to give me a chance to speak if I want. I'm ready for her to wrap this up, to say amen. She intakes a breath.

At the same time, I feel Naomi move to my right. "Dear God— " my daughter's voice is quiet and somber " —my mommy's still mad at You and doesn't want to talk to You."

"Naomi," I whisper.

With more force, she says, "Please help my mommy and daddy, all of us, when the bad men come. Help Atticus and Axel keep their ranch so they can have lots of cattle and make things good for everyone. Amen."

With tears stinging my eyes, I let out a quiet amen. "Thank you, Naomi."

She looks at me with a furrowed brow. "For what?"

"For asking God to help us."

"He will help us. Sebastian used to say God could talk to us if we listen. I listened—with my heart. He's going to help us. I know He will."

Chapter 20

Kimba

The sun has set, but it's far from dark, thanks to the waning full moon. The illumination will enable us to see the invaders coming in, but that goes both ways. Rey, Nicole, and their team will be visible as they sneak on to Brower's ranch and into his palatial home.

"Okay, so we're clear on the plan?" Rey asks as he meets the gaze of each person in our group.

After a few questions are answered, it's time to go. My group, consisting of Victoria, Jameson, Naomi, Patti, and her two children, will set up in the hideout. Rey, Nicole, and Brett will meet up with Axel and Atticus to go to Brower's mansion.

About half an hour ago, right on schedule, Rey checked in with Brower's men over the walkie-talkie, using the poor reception to help disguise his voice. He, Atticus, and Axel stayed in the watchers' location, sniper rifle at the ready, in case they didn't buy the ruse. Atticus and Axel are still there, watching and waiting for Rey's signal.

"I don't know what kind of reception we'll have, but I'll click the radio three times once we're in place," Rey says.

My heart's hammering in my chest. I want to tell him again to forget it, to bag this mission and move everyone to Simms. I open my mouth, but no words come out.

He gives me a weak smile. "We'll be okay. Nicole—she'll be okay."

My head bobs as if on a string. "She has to be okay. You . . . all of you."

Rey puts his hand on my bicep as his eyes delve into mine. "I love you."

Blinking away tears, I answer with a nod. I want to tell him the same, tell him I love him too. I do love him. But the words stick behind the lump in my throat. The wall between us is too large to scale with a simple word. My voice comes out thick. "I'll see you soon."

I turn to Nicole and wrap her in a hug.

"Too tight, Mom."

I loosen slightly but don't let her go. "Do everything exactly as your dad says. He knows how to keep you safe."

"No prob. We went over the plan a dozen times, maybe more, while we worked on the IEDs."

"Are you sure you're ready? If you aren't, just say so."

"Ready?" She gives a combination of a shrug and a shake of her head. "I know what to do. We all know what to do."

"You have your knife?"

"Both of them. You helped me with my weapons check, remember?"

I choose to ignore her sass, assuming it's the nervousness talking. I step back slightly to meet her eyes. "That's my girl."

She rolls her eyes, then smirks and shakes her head. "I guess. Um . . . I'll see you soon?"

"Absolutely."

While I'm talking with Nicole, Rey does the same with Naomi while Victoria is with Brett.

Once all the goodbyes are said, we start extinguishing lights. We'll leave a battery-operated lantern in the front room, but all the candles and oil lamps are put out. Burning down the ranch would defeat the purpose.

Rey and I discussed creating an incendiary substance out of some old, soured gas and a stash of packing peanuts. It could make a great diversion or buy my group time to escape. But the mixture could burn for hours, and the heat could ignite the surrounding foliage. Even though it was a wet spring, things are too dry now to risk it.

As we move toward the front door, Rey grabs my hand. The squeeze he gives it conveys a lifetime of emotions. A lifetime of memories. Of love.

I meet his eyes. "Come back."

His nod is somber. Determined. He gives me another squeeze before releasing. "Let's roll." He and his team slip out the door and into the night.

Lifting my chin, I turn to Naomi. "Nice and quiet as we walk to the hideout. Patti, give us a few minutes before you follow. Then, Victoria, you and LJ wait for five minutes after Patti leaves. Jameson— "

"I wait ten after Mom goes."

"Exactly."

Spreading out like this probably isn't necessary. Rey didn't see the need for his group, feeling it's better if they all go together. He assured me several times that no one else is watching. The two they dispatched were it. Not only did the men indicate they were the only ones during their conversation, but Rey glassed and scanned the entire area. Even so, this caution feels right.

At the fort, Patti is putting the kids down to sleep, nursing Trish and rubbing LJ's back, when Jameson makes his way up the hill and steps into the hideout.

"You left the light on?" I ask, keeping my voice low.

"Yep, just like you said. Left the front door unlocked also."

We discussed how to leave the houses. When Scott left the main house, he didn't lock the door, intentionally telling Atticus he was leaving it open. Not locking the doors seems like the best way to prevent damage to the houses.

After all, once this is over, the Dosens and Dawsons will be living here on the ranch, and Patti will at least be staying the winter before continuing on to her family's house in western Montana.

Our hope is Brower's men will come in all sneaky like and then, when they notice we aren't there, head back to Brower's place where Rey has already finished up. Once the crew finds out Lance Brower is dead, we think most of them will scatter, realizing this gig is over. A few will fight, hopefully very few.

The babies are asleep when the radio clicks three times. Rey and Nicole are in place, watching and waiting. He'll click once when he sees them leave. When he knows how many attackers are headed toward the Double D, he'll click off that count. Then he'll send over info on which way they're heading.

Because we took the radios off the men Rey and Atticus dispatched, we know the frequency they're using. We use a different channel, but it's still important to be cautious and maintain radio silence.

Rey will use Morse code to indicate the route they're taking. I learned Morse years ago as part of my operations training, and we also used it with the Bakerville security team, but I'm not completely fluent in it.

Rey wrote me a cheat sheet, which I'll use my red pen light to read. I'll really only need to make sure I get the first letter to know which way they're heading. Ideally, they'll all stick together and choose the river. Our traps and surprises along the way will surely slow them down.

After Rey sends the intel and the attackers are out of sight, his team will make their move. I squeeze my eyes shut and remember his hand holding mine, his blue eyes conveying his thoughts.

Okay, God, I'm giving You another chance. Show me You care about me, about us. Bring my husband and daughter back to me.

Chapter 21

Nicole

My heart's pounding so loud I'm surprised my dad doesn't give me the look—the one that says, "Maintain complete silence." He has lots of looks and gestures, so many we could probably carry on an entire conversation without using words.

I see my mom and him do it all the time. At least they used to. They were so in sync, they just seemed to know what the other was thinking with the raise of an eyebrow or the slight movement of their head.

These days, my mom barely looks at Dad. When she speaks to him, her voice is either monotone and emotionless or clipped with anger. He's not much better, communicating in single syllables and grunts more often than not.

I understand they're struggling since Nate died. We all are. But the way Mom blames Dad is wrong, especially since he blames himself too. He and Nate shared a tent, but the night of the storm, Dad was on watch. Nate was alone. I know he believes if he'd been in there, it would've been enough weight to keep the tent from going airborne.

Mom's blame toward Dad isn't about him being on watch instead of being with Nate. It's deeper than that. She blames him for us being here at all, for not being safe in Bakerville, maybe even for leaving Denver in the first place.

I don't dare point out to her how she's the one who told Dad we should keep our commitment to the Dosens—a commitment made last summer when we first met them in the small town of Meeteetse, Wyoming. We agreed then to help the family get home.

At the time, the plan was for us to go to Bozeman where family friends Chad and Beverly live, then the Dosens could finish the journey to Great Falls and their ranch on their own.

Things changed somewhere between then and when the travel plans started, with us getting them all the way home and then going on to Bozeman. The new plans began to form around the time we learned of the country's rebuilding efforts, and all of us—especially my mom—wanted to be a part of it, to be a part of history.

From the time of the EMP at the end of June until the middle of February, we'd heard little about what was happening in other parts of the country. There were rumors, of course, along with news shared by travelers. But never anything official. We didn't know if the government was still standing, if the president was alive . . . nothing.

Truthfully, we still don't know much. Even after the occasional radio announcement and conversations with soldiers in different places, it seems to be more hearsay than fact. Most say the entire planet is a mess, an undeclared World War III.

I don't know. All I know is what's happening here, the things I might have to do before the night is over. I might have to kill. Kill or be killed.

Mom gave me a pep talk earlier while she helped me with my weapons check. "Use the fear, Nicole. Let your body feel what it feels. You can't control it, but you can harness it. Use it along with your training to do what needs to be done."

I take a deep breath, focusing on my training and what will happen next. We're in place, well-hidden, with an excellent view of Brower's spread. The ginormous house is lit up. His solar system's working overtime to power what may be every light fixture. There's a flurry of activity with people going in and out. The many outbuildings, smaller cabins, and even a few outfitter's tents have people scampering about.

My parents said Brower's people wouldn't attack until around daylight, which is still several hours away. Are they planning to go earlier?

As if reading my mind, in a low voice, Dad says, "Bit of a circus. It might play out differently than we were thinking."

A horse lets out a low-pitched whinny, cattle bellow, a dog barks, someone yells at the dog to shut its trap.

I glance to the others with me, their faces illuminated by the light of the full moon. Axel's mouth is a tight line, his eyes hard and unyielding. Brett's face reflects the fear and apprehension I feel. Atticus is emotionless, staring at Brower's compound. My dad has the binoculars up, scanning from left to right.

We sit in silence, watching Brower's men scurry around like little ants. Not just men. Even from this distance, I think I see a woman or two among the group. Mom said Brower has cooks, housekeepers, and gardeners, which, from what she and Dad witnessed, are mostly women. But she didn't say anything about women working with the raiders.

My job will be to keep the household staff sleeping in the basement out of the way. Mom and Dad, with the Dosen brothers' help, put together a detailed blueprint of the house.

My parents toured the main floor and second floor when here earlier in the day, but not the basement. Both Atticus and Axel have been downstairs. Back then, it was just the cook and a housekeeper who lived in the basement apartments. There was also a game room, wine cellar, and other family spaces where they'd hung out with Connor a few times before the animosity between the parents became too severe.

EJ Martin, the ranch foreman, has a small house of his own, plus there's a second guest house on the grounds. There're also several small one or two-room cabins used by the other ranch hands. Now, with the increase of staff, we really have little idea where everyone's staying. We assume all the people who work in the home live in the basement, an assumption which may prove deadly.

I'll be stationed at the top of the staircase off the kitchen. Atticus says the stairs used to open to a large game room and it has a wide passage without a door. There's a second, narrower set of stairs on the other end of the house with a door. We'll lock that one and put Axel in a spot he can see both upstairs and downstairs.

While Axel and I take care of the main level and the staff, Atticus will be upstairs, where Brower's children sleep. The hope is, what my dad needs to do will be done quietly enough that Declan, Tara, Connor, and the hired help will sleep right through it. Scott, too, since he's probably with Tara.

Brett will stay here, where we're sheltered, acting as overwatch. He has one of the hunting rifles to make long shots. Axel and I have the shotguns, along with our sidearms—both visible ones and backups—plus our knives. Atticus and my dad have the tactical rifles along with sidearms and knives.

We'll go in quiet, using the large patio doors at the back for our entrance. Once everyone is in place, Dad will silently take care of Lance Brower, using the knife while we stand guard. When Brower is dead, Dad will go to the second floor to eliminate the oldest son.

Declan—or Mouth, as everyone except Lance Brower calls him—is just too much like his dad.

Dad won't kill Connor or Tara unless it's necessary. I hope it won't be. While I didn't think much of the brief interaction with Tara last night, Connor seemed nice, and he was saddened by the death of Asher and the other Dosens.

We're here maybe twenty minutes when the scurrying around seems to slow. One by one, lights are extinguished and things begin to calm down.

Dad leans close to me. "Relax. Try to sleep. I want you sharp when it's time to go."

I shake my head. "No way I can sleep."

"Try." He instructs the boys to rest also. He'll stay on watch and wake everyone when things look like they're getting going.

I lean against my go-pack, using it as a cushion in combination with a boulder. Dad and Mom had scoped out this area earlier, when going to see Brower. It's a similar location as Brower's men were using to watch us.

Even though I was sure I wouldn't be able to sleep, I wake with a start when something touches my arm. With the brightness of the moon, I can clearly see Dad holding up a finger, motioning me to remain silent. I give a nod.

The boys are already awake, watching as people begin streaming out of buildings. Atticus and Axel look tense, while Brett seems to have moved from frightened to determined. I set my jaw and push down my apprehension. This is happening—soon.

From our position, we can't see the front door of the mansion, but the layout of the smaller homes and cabins is excellent. A group of Brower's men make their way to one of the barns.

When we discussed earlier what would likely happen, how we thought they'd go about attacking the Double D, Mom and Dad both believed they'd go in on foot. With the ranches so close to each other, it doesn't make sense to take the horses. And because of the noise, it certainly wouldn't make sense to take the convertible or one of the pickup trucks. Most likely, they'll walk along the river and maybe the road.

But now, here they are by the barn and horse corral. My stomach churns, thinking they're going to ride in and take the river trail.

They'll encounter our traps.

Even though we made a point of not using anything fatal there, the horses could be injured by the snare or net. And the IEDs we've set up, not along the river but on game trails that could be used to attack my mom, those are set up to blow shrapnel into a human's legs. It'll do the same to the horses. A feeling of sickness starts in my belly.

The group enlarges. Clustered together, it's hard to tell how many there are. My mom needs the numbers so she knows what to expect. The plan is for her, Naomi, and the others to stay hidden and out of sight so the attackers believe we set the booby traps and fled, but the more info she has the better.

I let out a relieved breath when it's obvious the group is just using the corral as a meeting place instead of saddling the horses. The moonlight glints off several long guns slung on their backs, ready to put to use. They're still too bunched together, too close to get an accurate count.

My heart's pounding again, the adrenaline pumping. I let out a breath through my nose and focus on the group, waiting for them to spread out so we can count. Minutes later, they cooperate, moving one or two at a time away from the barn and toward the driveway.

"Seventeen," Atticus says when they've stopped and clumped up again.

I nod my agreement.

"Wait." Dad holds up his hand. "Let's see what happens next."

What happens next reminds me of being on the playground, dividing up to play an impromptu game of soccer. One of the men starts pointing and moving people into groups.

Atticus groans. "Worst case scenario."

Within a few minutes, a group of ten head off toward the river. Four take the road, while three others go overland and make a beeline for the fence dividing Brower's spread and the Double D.

Dad clicks the radio, sending the info to my mom of how many men total and then how many are going on each path. As soon as he's finished, he leans back and lets out a frustrated breath. "These folks can't be counted on to do what we expect. I sure hope this thing doesn't go south."

Chapter 22

Kimba

As the long-awaited clicks of the radio keep sounding off, it's clear things aren't what we hoped. Seventeen tangos are coming from all three directions.

We're outgunned for sure. Jameson and me each have a .308 rifle. Victoria has the high-capacity .22, while Patti has her .243. If we're discovered, Jameson and Patti will bug out with the children while Victoria and I hold off the attackers. I hope it doesn't come to that.

Even in a somewhat fortified and elevated position, the two of us against such a group has less than stellar odds. Add in Victoria not squeezing a trigger but twice in almost twenty years, and it definitely doesn't look good. Hopefully, the traps along the riverbank and the few IEDs strategically placed en route to the hideout gives us a slight advantage to help even the playing field.

Earlier, Victoria, Patti, and I found not only a secondary hideout where we've stashed a few other goodies, but also a third position should the secondary fall. And if everything goes to pot, the fourth and final convergence is the town of Simms, four miles away.

Rey and Nicole, along with the others, also know each of the hideouts and meeting spots. Once they've successfully completed their mission, they know where to find us.

My gaze moves to Naomi, leaning against a boulder at the back of the shelter. She's sound asleep with a peaceful smile on her face.

Patti scoots next to me. "Seventeen? Was that the count?"

I respond with a grim nod. "Coming from each direction." I let out a long breath through my nose and count to eight. "Let's get a jump on things. I want you to go on to the secondary hideout. If things go bad, Victoria and I will lead them across the road to the large rock outcropping. You remember it from earlier?"

"The one we considered as our secondary?"

I nod. "You'll be able to see us from there and will know if you need to get out. You'll be able to get to the next fallback location without being seen. Just be completely quiet." I glance at the sleeping babies. They've been great on this journey. Even Trish, who is still so young, rarely makes a peep.

She gives a nod. "Go now? You want us to— "

"Go now." I puff out a breath before turning to Jameson. "You ready?"

His face is pale in the moonlight, and his nodded response is grim.

"Victoria, you and Jameson keep watch. We have time before they reach us. I'm going to wake up Naomi and tell her . . ." I wave my hand as I lean my rifle against the boulder.

Kneeling by my daughter's side, my eyes begin to sting. She's so perfect, so beautiful and full of life. I know Patti will care for her as if she's her own. And Jameson, though things started out less than stellar with him on this journey, is becoming a fine young man. He'll stand with Patti and do what's needed to help keep the children safe.

I lean in and inhale her scent. Thanks to a sponge bath earlier today, even washing her hair, she smells fresh and clean. *Childlike.* I drop a gentle kiss on her forehead.

Her eyes flutter a few times before popping open. She pulls her lips together and gives a stretch.

I put my finger to my mouth. "Shh."

"Are they coming?" she asks in a hushed tone.

"They are. Patti's taking you to the other hideout. I'll be there soon."

She furrows her brow. "I'll help with the babies."

"I know you will. Grab your pack, and you can carry the sleeping mat, okay?"

"Jameson?"

"He'll be with you." I give her another kiss.

Patti already has Trish snug against her chest in the baby wrap. LJ is awake, standing sleepily next to his mom as she rolls the sleeping mat and secures it with a small bungee cord.

"Give me a hug," I say to Naomi.

With her tight in my arms, I savor the feel of her, just like I did with Nicole earlier. Like I wish I would've done with Rey. I release Naomi and turn to Patti. "Keep a good watch. Be ready to move again."

Patti gives a solemn nod as she hands Naomi the mattress. She motions to Jameson. "Ready?"

"Bye, Mommy," Naomi whispers as they move out the back of our hideout. They scamper across the flat top and begin down the other side. As soon as my daughter's blond hair is out of sight, I allow my shoulders to drop. I take a deep breath before returning to my watch station.

Back in the overwatch position, Victoria gives a sad shake of her head, her eyes wet with unshed tears. As I was saying goodbye to my youngest child, she was saying goodbye to hers. Now we wait. Wait for the invaders. Wait until this is over and our families can be reunited.

Chapter 23

Nicole
Saturday, August 8

Once the attackers are out of sight, we're ready to move toward the mansion. My knees feel like jelly, and my heart's pounding in my ears.

Brett gives me a thumbs up. "You've got this, Nicole. You'll be fine."

My return smile is less than confident. I may have trained for this, but it still feels wrong. As part of the Bakerville militia, we practiced breaching houses. I'm competent not only with the firearms and knife but also in hand-to-hand combat. We've kept up our training as we've traveled, running drills with the guns and practicing martial arts.

I know how to defend myself, and so do the Dosen boys. And my dad—well, he's a well-trained combatant. A professional.

We know the bulk of Brower's men have left. He may have a security guard or two, though Mom and Dad didn't see anyone earlier today when they had the tour of the house. We can do this. We'll get it done and then go to the Double D and help Mom.

That's the plan.

I refuse to think about the number of times our plans have gone wrong.

As we approach the house, Dad motions to the full wall of glass. We're going in the back, entering through the glass doors in the informal family room. As I go over the plan, I try and remember the crude blueprint Mom and Dad drew of the house to show us where everything is.

Dad'll pick the lock, then we'll clear the common areas of the main level. I'll go to my post by the basement access. Axel will be at the front of the house, watching the main staircase and the secondary basement access while Dad and Atticus clear the open areas upstairs. Dad will leave Atticus there while he returns to the main level and does what's needed to stop Lance Brower for good.

We can do this. It'll work as it should. Please, God, make it so.

The brothers and I take a knee and provide cover for Dad while he jimmies the lock. He motions success with his hand. We quickly move next to him, stacking up by the door. I'll go left, Atticus right, Dad will go straight and low, and Axel straight and high.

"Go," Dad whispers as he pops the door.

We're all in when the room lights up.

"Thought we might see you here," a low voice announces. "I didn't buy the hayseed routine for a minute. Put the weapons down and let's have a chat."

A growl emits from my dad.

"Scott?" Atticus's voice is filled with disbelief. "W-why?"

"Guns down. Now."

Dad lets out another growl. "Do it. Put them down."

I lower the muzzle of my shotgun. In my peripheral, I see the others do the same. My gaze is focused on Scott, who's holding a pistol on us. He's joined by another man—older with an overly lined face—a woman of about the same age with dull gray hair pulled into a bun, and half a dozen others. Connor Brower, Atticus's and Axel's so-called friend, rounds out the group. All are armed.

"Where's Brower?" Dad asks.

"Gone." Scott motions slightly with the pistol. "He and Mouth went with the raiders. They took the road. Said he's walking in with his head held high, just like he owns the place. Mouth's with him, as well as two of the worst, most ruthless of the gang."

My stomach clenches. It was a setup, the entire thing.

"Where's the rest of your people?" the old man asks.

Dad lifts his chin. "Safe."

The man and Scott look at each other.

"They're in the fort, aren't they?" Scott asks. "Where you boys used to play?"

My eyes go wide. He knows. He knows where my mom is. My little sister. The babies. I feel sick to my stomach.

"Why are you doing this, Connor?" Axel's voice drips with disappointment.

"We're done, finished with the way things are. My dad and brother . . ." The young man swallows hard, his Adam's apple bobbing. "They've lost their minds. Tara too."

"Wait." I shake my head. "What's happening here?"

Scott lowers his pistol, and the others follow suit.

"What *is* happening here?" Dad asks.

Connor looks to the others in his group. "We're ending it. Scott said you'd have a plan and would probably attack here. We figured if you did, we'd join forces with you and stop this madness. Try to take my dad into custody and turn him and Mouth over to the . . . to someone. Bring them to justice."

The old man gives a single bob of his head. "We need to move. I've got men with Brower, part of the raiders. They're waiting for my signal."

I suck in my top lip, trying to sort things out.

"You're with us?" Axel asks, directing a hard gaze at Connor. "You're going against your dad?"

Lance Brower's youngest son has a pained look on his face. "It has to happen. My dad can't continue with what he's doing. Will you help us?"

"D-dad?" I stutter out his name.

He takes a step forward. "Let's do it."

"Are you sure?" Axel asks. "It could be a trick."

"Why?" He looks to Axel. "If they wanted us dead, they'd have already done it. Let's move. Let's finish this."

The old man barks out orders, telling everyone to grab their gear. He turns to the gray-haired lady standing next to him. "There shouldn't be any trouble here."

"We'll be fine. Just— " She gives him a tender look. "I'd like to have you come back to me, Eustace Martin."

He puts a worn hand against her cheek. "You'd better believe it." After an intense moment, he pulls away. "Keep them tied up, no matter how much crying and carrying on they do."

"Leave who tied up?" I ask.

Their eyes dart to me. Heat warms my face as I realize they know I've witnessed their affection.

The old man, Eustace Martin, steps toward me. "Tara Brower and a couple others loyal to Lance. We've secured the three in a room. She— " He shakes his head.

The woman makes a clicking noise with her tongue. "The girl thinks her daddy walks on water."

"Now, Twila . . ." Eustace gives the woman a wink.

"It's true! As far as she's concerned, he can do no wrong. She's not like Connor. He's . . ." She contorts her mouth. "He knows right from wrong. Those other two, though . . ."

I give a nod and turn to the man. "How'd you know we'd be here, Eustace?"

His mustache twitches. "Eustace? Ain't no one but Twila calls me that. My name's EJ. EJ Martin."

"Oh. I, uh . . . is EJ short for Eustace something?"

Twila snorts out a laugh. "EJ's short for something, but he won't say what. I decided Eustace fits him."

"We'd better get a move on," Scott says. "Everyone know what they're doing? You have your weapons and gear?"

There's a minute or so of scrambling as last-minute preparations are made. Several others who weren't with the group when they caught us sneaking in have now joined. Scott and EJ go over the loose plan they've made.

Dad asks a few questions and offers suggestions.

One, a woman not much older than me, is decked out in black pants and a top, wearing a utility belt and looking fierce; she says she's ready to go. Twila, a man in his late twenties or early thirties, and three women are staying behind.

"We're taking the road and going through the field," Scott says. "My guess is those in Brower's group taking the river path may meet a few obstacles." Scott's eyes meet Atticus's.

"A few," Atticus agrees. "And don't use the game trails behind the houses or along the ridgeline. We set up a few, um . . ." He looks to my dad.

"Ambushes. Potentially fatal." Dad spends a few seconds detailing where the IEDs are and how they need to avoid them. He turns to Connor. "We'll do our best to take your dad and brother alive. But there's no— "

Connor raises a hand. "I know. Scott and EJ told me. No guarantees. I understand."

Dad gives a single dip of his head. "I'll get a message to my wife. She needs to know there are friendlies coming in."

"So they didn't leave?" Scott hefts his backpack into place.

"She's safe, waiting."

Scott gives a wry smile. "I knew it. I knew the whole thing was an act. Let's move, folks, double time so we can get there before anything happens. Brower wanted everyone in place, waiting for the sun to rise."

Scott turns to my dad again. "Your wife's in the boys' fort? It's a good spot. With the sun coming up behind her, it'll help with concealment and give her an advantage."

"That's right."

"Good plan."

Scott walks us from the family room through a hallway and into an all-white living room, where two more men are waiting. When we step out the front door of the palatial home and on to the paved circular drive, the band of light on the horizon encourages us to hurry.

I'm at the back of the group, walking next to the woman decked out in black. "You're Nicole?" she asks.

I answer with a nod.

"I'm Annie, one of the housekeepers."

Turning my head to give her a smile, I notice a flapping by her foot. "Your boot's untied."

She makes a noise of disgust in her throat. "Stupid slippery laces. I've already redone it several times this morning."

"Are they new?" I motion to the shiny black boot with the flopping lace.

Annie nods before kneeling. "I didn't have anything suitable for this."

"I hope they're broken in. You don't want a blister."

A shadow crosses her face. "Um, no. Not really. Someone found them." She looks back down and gives the shoestring a yank. "You don't have to wait for me. I can catch up."

I lift a shoulder and half turn to see how far behind we are. The rest of the group is on the other side of the tall hedge. I can see heads popping up and down as they walk. As I turn back toward Annie, there's a blur of movement as she lets out an *oomph*.

Annie's on the ground, with a woman standing over her.

The woman's eyes meet mine as she lifts her arm and swings it in a downward arc. The glint of steel catches on the moonlight as the knife embeds to the hilt into Annie's throat. I move the shotgun up to shoot and open my mouth to yell when an arm comes around my neck, yanking hard.

My scream turns into a gurgle as the shotgun flies from my hands.

I move my now empty hands to the strong forearms, attempting to protect my neck from the chokehold. With my heart pounding, I step forward and plant my left foot solidly on the ground.

I turn into my attacker, slipping my shoulder and body low as I face him. I have time to register his height—over a full head taller than me—as I push my hands into his stomach to gain space between us.

A look of surprise covers his pockmarked face. I lift a foot and give a solid kick to his gut, sending him to the ground. He lands on his butt with a solid thump.

I pull my pistol as I step to the side. I don't want my back to the woman with the knife. From the side of my eye, I register Annie's crumpled body. The woman isn't there.

The man's lip curls.

"Stop!" I yell, my gun raised toward him.

He lets out a roar as he scrambles to his feet.

I squeeze the trigger, and he flinches.

I pop off another round, this one hitting him in the shoulder, spinning him halfway. He lets out a yelp as he goes to the ground.

Looking for the missing woman, I step toward Annie. Her glassy eyes stare at me. The knife, like her attacker, is gone.

"Nicole!" my dad calls out.

"I'm here. There's . . . it's clear." I'm sick to my stomach, struggling to keep my weapon trained on the man as he squirms on the ground, one hand pushed into his ruined shoulder.

Dad, Atticus, and Axel, along with a couple of others from Scott's group, cautiously approach from the hedge.

"There's someone else," I say as I point to the man on the ground. "A woman. She killed— " I motion to Annie as my stomach recoils again.

"Was it Tara?" Scott's face is pale as he kneels next to the dead girl.

"Not her." I shake my head. "This woman was older."

"Sidney—she worked in the gardens. She was tied up with Tara and Derek."

"Where'd she go?" Axel asks.

"Probably to warn Brower," Dad says. "Let's go. No need to be stealthy now. We need to use your truck, go in quick and hard. If Sidney overheard us, they know where my wife is." He pulls the radio from his belt. "We're done with radio silence too."

My stomach does another flip. Scott called Mom's hideout the fort. Could Brower know where it is? Did Tara overhear? If so, my mom and sister are in danger.

Chapter 24

Kimba

The radio makes a clicking noise before crackling to life. The signal is weak, the voice garbled and incomprehensible. My heart rate accelerates. Even muddled, I know it's Rey. He's broken radio silence. Something has changed.

"Overwatch Two, copy." Brett's voice comes in loud and clear.

Victoria gives a trill of relief. I send her a quick smile and press the talk button. "Repeat for Overwatch One."

Another crackle and garbled transmission. After a pause, Brett says, "They're coming. Brower's with them. They may know about you. Help is on the way. Be ready for anything."

"Wh-what does that mean?" Victoria shakes her head. "Why is Brower with them?"

I tilt my head, relieving the stress in my neck. "I don't know, but we were smart to send Patti and the children away."

A whimper escapes her as she stiffens. I glance in her direction and meet her brown eyes. They're hard. Determined. She dips her head. "Then we'll do what we must."

"Remember, your .22 may seem like a child's toy, especially with my rifle booming next to it, but the Ruger has a BX-25 magazine. You've got twenty-six rounds with the one in the chamber, plus backup magazines. And you know how to slap in the new mag, right?"

"Right. I'm good." She looks anything but as she straightens her shoulders. "I have another twenty-five round mag and a ten round. I . . . I can do what's needed. I *will* do what's needed."

"Good. While my Mossberg .308 may have more firepower, I have a five-round magazine and only one backup. I'll be choosing my shots and relying on you to keep me covered when I need to change out."

"Plus, we each have our sidearms." She touches her hip.

For the entirety of our journey from Wyoming, Victoria has been unarmed except for a pair of axes on her hips. It's only since a couple of nights ago, when she shot the grizzly bear with Jennifer's handgun, she's switched to having firepower.

The trouble is, she hasn't shot but one of the guns. Jennifer's .357 Magnum revolver, which Victoria used to shoot the bear, is concealed in an inside holster at her kidney. She also has a semi-auto on her right hip. She dry fired both earlier, and she's demonstrated she knows how to handle them and the .22 rifle.

But it's all theoretical. The rest of us have spent hours practicing—running drills, dry firing, shooting with both dominate and weak hands, drawing our main weapons and our backups, and much more.

Victoria doesn't have any of that. She didn't drill with us; she didn't do any of the hand-to-hand combat training. She's well beyond her depth of knowledge. Hearing her history, how she learned to shoot as a child growing up in the Appalachian Mountains, gives me hope she'll know what to do and won't crumble under pressure.

"If everything goes pear-shaped, you know what to do. Just remember, the handguns don't have the distance."

"And I have my ax." She motions to her left hip, reminding me of her proficiency with the heavy blade. "You have your knives."

"Let's hope no one is close enough we need to use them."

"Amen to that."

A scream pierces the night.

Her eyes go wide. "What— "

A smile plays at my lips. "Seems like someone may have found one of our river path surprises."

She lifts her chin. "Serves them right." After a few beats of silence, she whispers, "I . . . I hate this, hate we're forced to kill. There's been too much violence already. We came here to live in peace, to start fresh."

A beam of light filters through the trees along the river. "Looks like they're giving up traveling in darkness. Let's keep quiet and be ready. Remember, we do not engage unless they force us to."

"Are the bombs in the right spots?"

"The IEDs are fine."

The flashlight bobs along, stopping every few feet. We're well into twilight. The sun has yet to peek up behind us, but there's enough light to make things out.

My gaze roams over the ranch, searching the fence line that divides the Brower and Dosen properties. I move to the paved road and skirt the hills—where we saw the heads bobbing earlier today as they were on their way to watch us—then back to the trees along the river where the light still marks their progress.

"Someone's there." Victoria lifts her chin toward the property line where the beginning of sunlight catches on glass.

As quick as we see him, he disappears. I raise my binoculars to search him out. It takes only a few seconds to find not only him but two more. All three are lying prone, weapons trained on the houses.

"That's the right amount," I whisper. "Rey's code said three were coming overland. Four on the road. Ten along the river."

"And Brower's with them. Which group?" she asks, her voice laced with nervousness.

"Don't know. It doesn't matter too much. We're just watching and helping our people when they arrive. It'll be . . ." I take in a breath through my nose. "Things will be fine."

The flashlight along the river goes out. Is there enough light they can now see the surprises we left for them? Maybe. We can see clearly now, but I'd expect it to be darker in the trees.

"Keep an eye on our friends along the fence line," I say. "I'm going to watch for the river people to come into view."

"The waiting . . ." Victoria shakes her head. "My heart's pounding so loud I can barely think."

"It's okay to be nervous. *Fearful.* We just can't allow the fear to stop us from doing what we must."

As we wait, soft pink light bathes the ranch. Another dawn and what I'm sure will be a beautiful sunrise—my favorite time of day. I wish I could enjoy it and bask in the beauty of a new day.

I crinkle my forehead. The snipers are in place, but those along the river have yet to appear. I expected the attack to occur before full light, yet here we are. Sunrise is probably less than twenty minutes away.

If they were smart, they'd have made their move when the light was just enough to make things out, to be able to distinguish the buildings and see movement. Get in and get it done, hit hard while people are still sleeping.

I look to the road and try to find the group coming that way. There's no movement, no sign of anyone. Rey's team should be here soon.

A feeling of dread starts low in my stomach. My legs suddenly feel weak. Something isn't right. The hair stands up on the back of my neck.

"Hello, Mrs. Hoffmann."

I spin around, and Victoria lets out a gasp.

"I know, I know. You're surprised to see me." Lance Brower lifts his hands, a much too large smile covering his tanned face. His son is next to him with his pistol trained on us, held in a sideways grip. Two more men are behind them, standing in the open area at the back of our hideout.

"Almost ruined my surprise with your trip wire there. Good thing my men know about these things and helped me avoid them."

I glance to the men behind him. One's wearing a red ballcap and holding a carbine; I labeled him yesterday as their main killer. His face is emotionless, his eyes dead. The guy next to him is wearing a smug grin, his mustache twitching and his cowboy hat and pistol bobbing.

"Imagine my surprise when my daughter told me she overheard where you were hiding." Brower purses his lips as he strokes his chin. "I must say, I'm mildly surprised to see you holding a rifle. From our interaction yesterday, I'd understood you to be a passivist."

Slipping back into the Kim persona, I give him a seductive smile. "I am. It's just my watch time. We all take turns. While the others are sleeping, Ruby and me— " I motion toward Victoria " —we're on watch. Where's your daughter? I'd love to say hello."

Mouth snorts out a laugh. "Sure you would."

Brower raises his hand, motioning toward his son. "Is that right? So . . . your husband and the others at my house, they're . . . what? Sleepwalking?"

Mouth throws back his head this time, making a weird chuckling noise. "Sleepwalking. Good one, Dad."

Lance Brower's eyes go hard. "Where's the kids?"

I lift my chin and drop my shoulders. *Show's over.* "Safe."

"Humph. Don't bet on it. You two, put your rifles on the ground."

Victoria looks toward me.

I give a slight nod as I slowly lean to my right and prop the Mossberg against the boulder.

"Good. Now the handguns. Nice and slow. You do anything I don't like, and my men will shoot your friend. What'd you say her name is? Ruby? Ruby's as good as dead if you so much as twitch wrong."

As I move my hand to my sidearm, there's sudden chaos as the roar of an engine breaks the silence. The armed men react to the threat, their weapons seeking out new targets.

I shove my shoulder into Victoria, sending her toward the rocks on the other side of our hideout. As she scrambles in that direction, I unholster my gun. As soon as it's clear of the holster and aimed in the general direction of Brower and his men, I fire and move away from Victoria.

As I scurry behind a much too small boulder, Victoria's gun echoes through the hideout. She's shooting a 9-millimeter Springfield Armory with 13+1 rounds on tap. The way she's firing, she'll be empty in seconds.

While she has their attention, I switch out my near empty mag for a fresh one.

I lean around the edge of the boulder. Brower and his son are nowhere in sight. The two men with them are sprawled on the ground, blood saturating the dirt.

I glance at Victoria. Her slide is open, her mouth an *O* as she clicks the release and lets the magazine fall to the ground. She slams another in place, smooth as clockwork. There's still shooting happening, coming from along the river and the houses. It's a crazy warzone.

Victoria's cover, which was good when Brower was shooting, doesn't work for threats from other directions. The guys on the property line, while some distance away, could get off a lucky shot. Hopefully, the sun coming up in their eyes is leaving them partially blind.

"Ruby," I hiss, using the name I made up for her.

Her eyes meet mine.

I mouth, *"Where's Brower?"*

She motions to the exit at the back with her chin. *"Gone,"* she mouths. *"I think I hit him. You got his kid."*

I purse my lips and motion for her to move toward me as I cover her. The two men bleeding on the dirt aren't getting up, but Brower could reappear at any moment. And he mentioned his daughter. Where is she?

With Victoria near me and protected from the shooters on the property line, I let out a breath. "Stay here. Use your .22 only if needed. We should assume Brower used the radio to tell them where we are. If you see them and they try to storm the hideout, you get out. Head for the high ground across the road, where Jameson and Patti will be able to see you from their shelter."

She answers with a wide-eyed nod.

"If you can, set up the IED at the back exit. Just connect the trip line like we talked about earlier, okay?"

"But if you come back— "

"I won't be coming back, not that way."

"Rey?"

"Nope." I pull out the radio. "Liberator, this is Overwatch One. Hideout is compromised. Do not approach. Repeat, hideout is compromised."

"Where are they?" Victoria asks. "I heard the truck and saw it out of the corner of my eye as it whipped around the corner."

"Our people?"

She lifts a shoulder. "I don't know. Things were crazy."

"Yeah. They still are. Keep your head down. Do what we discussed."

She flares her eyes.

"Keep the radio," I say, thrusting it in her direction. "If you don't hear from Rey shortly, make the same announcement again."

"Where are you going?"

"I'm going after Brower."

I have a full mag in my handgun. The mag I released earlier is in the dirt. There's at least one round still in it. I should take the time to reload, but I don't want to risk losing Brower—risk him finding Patti and the kids in the secondary hideout.

I shove the magazine in my pocket. I touch my ankle, feeling the backup gun there: my Glock 43, a gift from Doris Snyder before we left the mountain. The six-round magazine plus one in the chamber gives me even more firepower.

I grab my rifle before giving Victoria a final nod. I cautiously move toward the back of the hideout, keeping my gun trained toward the men on the ground. They haven't moved. I'm fairly certain they're dead, but I'm still being smart about this.

As I near the one in the red ballcap, my suspicion is confirmed. Part of his face is missing. The second's body is riddled with holes to his torso. I move around them and use the brush near the back exit for cover, staying low. Taking a deep breath, I dart out, pistol up.

Chapter 25

Nicole

"Nicole," Dad says as he thrusts the radio in my direction, "you've got communications. Brett's staying on overwatch. One of the men with Axel has a radio."

I answer with a nod. "We're just going up the road?"

"Going in hot, just like we own the place."

I give a slight smile and shake my head at Dad's duplication of how Scott said Lance Brower went in.

I pile into the bed of the old, rusted-out pickup truck as Atticus holds my shotgun. Dad climbs in the front seat, with Scott driving. Several of EJ's men are in the back with us.

It's already twilight as we start out, enough illumination to see clearly. We haven't heard any shooting and don't think they've started the attack. And we have no idea where Tara Brower or the killer Sidney went. We can only assume they've hurried away to meet up with Brower.

Axel led a group along the river. Since he set up most of the traps, he's the best to help EJ's men avoid them. EJ went with Axel, saying some of the men are loyal to him and are ready for this to end.

Connor Brower also went with the river group. One of EJ's men stayed back to render first aid on Derek, the man I shot. My dad said I shouldn't think about that now, to put it in a box and come back to it later. We have a job to do.

As we roar up the road and crest the hill, a ping sounds, followed by the repercussion of a gunshot.

"They're shooting at us!" someone yells.

I scootch down in the back of the truck. I have no idea where the shots are coming from. As the truck barrels up the road, it begins to swerve. Even if I had a target in sight, I wouldn't be able to return fire. As we reach the bottom of the hill, the shots keep coming.

The radio on my hip lets out a squeal, and I grab for it. The truck slides around the corner, leaving the pavement and drifting on the gravel driveway of the Double D. It doesn't straighten in time and clips the upright entrance logs.

I lose hold of the radio. It bounces on the metal of the truck bed and flitters toward the tailgate.

Crawling toward the radio, I'm kicked as one of the men adjusts his position.

"Watch it," he grunts.

When I reach the walkie-talkie, the back is off and the batteries are gone. I let out a growl.

"Hold on!" someone yells. "We're leaving the road."

I bounce up and come down hard on my side. A few more bounces and we skid to a stop.

"Nicole?" Atticus calls for me.

"I'm okay."

"You hit?"

"No. But the radio—I need to fix it."

He gives me a strange look and then bolts over the side of the pickup bed. "We've got the buildings for cover. Get the radio. I'll wait."

I'm the last in the truck. Three of the AA batteries are easy to find, the fourth is in the corner. My shaky hands make putting it back together a challenge.

"Ready?" Atticus asks, his voice clipped.

Even though the volleys have slowed, there's still shooting. I look toward the hideout where my mom and sister are. This close to the main house, nothing beyond is visible.

"Someone was calling. I heard it go off, but I don't know— "

"On the radio? Let's move to where your dad is. You can call them from there while I help take them out."

I grimace at his choice of words, as the image of Derek pops into my head. *Put it in a box.* I climb over the bed of the truck, using the wheel to help me reach the ground. The rest of our group has spread out.

Atticus points to the edge of the barn. We run bent over to my dad's side.

"What happened?" Dad asks when we reach him.

"I dropped the radio. They called us. I didn't hear."

"Ask for a repeat."

I move several feet from Dad and Atticus. With one knee on the ground, I click the radio three times before clearing my throat. "Repeat last for Liberator."

There're several beats of silence. I let out a long breath through my mouth, counting to four like my mom says helps her. I take in a breath through my nose, repeating the four counts.

I click the button again. "Liberator needs repeat of last transmissions. Repeat, Liberator did not copy."

"Lib . . . or . . . this . . . Two.   Overwatch . . . compromised. Approach . . . repeat . . ." the radio lets out a shriek.

"Hoffmann, Atticus." Scott's waving from his position by the main house.

"Dad!" I call. When he looks at me, I point to Scott. "He wants you. Atticus too."

Scott motions for them to move to him.

"Nicole, you're with me," Dad says. "Stay low and move quick."

We do a combination duck walk/sprint in the open area between the buildings. As soon as we reach safety, Dad asks, "The radio?"

"I don't know. Brett said something, but it wasn't clear. I didn't reach Mom."

"Try again." We sidle up to Scott. "What is it?"

"Look." Scott points toward the ridge behind us, on the east side of the ranch.

I squint into the morning sun. "What?"

"Movement. People, at least three."

"Why?"

Atticus says a word I've never heard him use. "They're going to the hideout, in the back. Our people— "

"Are sitting ducks," my dad finishes. "Nicole, radio."

With shaking hands, I pass it off to him. "Mom?"

He gives me a nod. "They'll get out." He clicks the radio once. "Overwatch One, escape. Escape. Go now!"

"We can't see them from here," I say.

"They'll get out," Dad repeats. "If we can see movement, they should've also."

I look to Atticus. He knows the place, having played there his entire life. "Is that true?"

His gaze is focused on the hillside. "I got them, the tangos." He quickly goes to his knee and pulls the tactical rifle against his shoulder. He stitches a seam of bullets into the terrain.

Scott joins in the shooting as my dad positions himself next to Atticus, his rifle also barking. I feel completely useless with the shotgun, which is no good at this distance. I consider using my pistol, but it wouldn't help either.

When they stop shooting, Scott says, "I'd say you got their attention."

"Yeah." Atticus nods. "But did we stop them?"

"Did you put any of your boobytraps up there?"

"Maybe one or two."

"Really? Where?"

A muffled bang and a puff of dirt, followed by a blood curdling scream, elicit a grunt from my dad. "Right about there."

My stomach clenches. One less person who can hurt my family and friends is good. I force myself not to think about what the shrapnel could've done to him. Dad said the loads wouldn't be fatal in a normal world.

With the way things are, where nothing is normal and there's not a real hospital . . . I shove the thoughts down. These people are trying to kill us. Shooting at us and—

Dirt puffs up a few inches from my dad. He quickly moves against the building.

"That's what I get for lollygagging."

"What do we do now?" Atticus asks, his eyes scanning for targets. The shooting behind us has slowed from a continual cadence to an occasional ping.

"We're moving to the other house."

As I arch my body, ready to move, the walkie-talkie sounds. "Liberator. This . . . Two."

Dad waits a moment to see if they say anything else. When they don't, he clicks his radio. "Overwatch Two, Overwatch One is compromised. Do you know if they got out? Over."

Brett says something, but it's so garbled we can't make it out.

Atticus motions with his hand. "Stupid radio. Doesn't work at all. We should've kept one of ours."

Dad tightens the antenna. "Then Brett or Kimba would have one not working."

Rolling his eyes, Atticus agrees with a nod.

"Say again, Overwatch Two."

We wait a few moments, but there's no response from Brett.

"Time to move," Dad says. "Scott— "

"Yep. I'll provide cover fire."

I pull my shotgun down to ready position. If someone comes out of nowhere, I want to be prepared.

"Go." The three of us take off at Dad's command. I'm running full speed, slightly hunched. I'm shocked when I reach the house without having heard any new gunfire.

Is this over?

No. Not until we're all back together—safe.

"There it is." Atticus points to the hideout. "I don't see anyone."

"Isn't that the purpose?" I ask.

He lifts a shoulder.

"I'm going up," my dad says. "I want you two to cover me from here."

"Dad— "

He gives me a slight smile. "It's fine. Cover me."

"Don't forget about the IED." Atticus motions to the hillside. "It's on the game trail. And they said they'd set one up at the back if they bugged out."

"I remember."

"Dad, they might . . . you could get shot."

"Not a chance. Your mom knows to identify first."

"But Victoria and Jameson . . ."

He turns to look at me full on. "Nicole, this is necessary."

My mouth's a tight line as I nod. "I could go in the house and get a rifle, come with you. We still have— "

"No time." He moves his hand to my cheek. "I love you, Blondie."

With Atticus covering him, he takes off fast and low.

"Do I help you cover?" I ask.

"Can you refill my magazine?" Atticus thrusts the black polymer mag in my direction, along with a fabric pouch of cartridges. "I only have one backup. If things go south— "

I nod my head and sling the shotgun on my back. As I start the job of reloading, the shooting ramps up again. "Are they shooting at my dad?" He's still moving, completely out in the open.

"I don't see the shooter," Atticus mutters.

My dad's only a few feet from where the incline begins when there's another poof of an explosion and a scream.

"Where was it?" I crane my head, furiously looking for the blast.

"There." Atticus points. "The hideout. They must have set the trip wire."

"That means— "

"They're out. They wouldn't have set it unless they were leaving. I'm sure of it."

Relief floods through me. They're out. They've left the hideout and went to the backup location. It should mean . . . it *must* mean they're okay. They'll be fine.

Chapter 26

Kimba

The percussion of a small explosion turns my head. My mouth goes dry. Another IED. One went off a few minutes ago, somewhere along the ridgeline. This one's closer. Victoria. Our hideout.

I scoot behind a dense thatch of brush. Victoria's instructions were to head for the rock outcropping across the highway and slightly east. With the sun now illuminating the land, I've been following a blood trail left behind by either Brower or his son, possibly both. My new objective is to take cover, watch for Victoria, and provide any necessary cover fire as she makes her way to safety.

A twinge of guilt runs through me. I shouldn't have left her. Going after Brower on my own was stupid. At the time, I thought finding them would be a quick endeavor. I'd get it done, stop the threat, and get back to her.

But Brower's proven to be elusive, slipping out of sight and leaving only sporadic splotches to follow. We may have hit them, but the injuries weren't enough to stop them. It barely even slowed them down.

Within seconds, Victoria comes into view. She's moving quick and steady, scanning the area as she goes. As I take a step out of the brush to call to her, another person comes into view.

"Stop right there!" a tall woman yells before popping off a shot.

Victoria spins, firing the rifle as she twists, stitching the ground in front of the woman. As my friend scurries to the brush, I fire at the tall woman and miss.

With a primordial growl, she turns in my direction and releases several wild shots. I shoot again, hitting her. She goes down.

A short woman with black hair steps out from the brush and lets out a guttural scream as she releases a volley of shots. My mind has time to register the shooter as Tara Brower. I move into deeper cover while her AR-15 tears up the trees around me.

A ping tells me Victoria is again shooting, her lightweight rifle with its tiny bullets producing enough energy to do some serious damage with the right hit.

Bladed against the trunk of the largest tree I can quickly find, I search for Tara Brower. She's out of sight and not shooting. Victoria's rifle is also silent.

The hair on the back of my neck stands at attention. I spin around at the breaking of a twig.

"Well, we meet again, Mrs. Hoffmann." Lance Brower has his handgun trained on my chest. "I must say, you're full of surprises. Toss the rifle aside—again."

At my hesitation, he growls, "Do what I say."

The tingling starts in my lips and hands, my chest begins to tighten. *Not now!* Breathing out through my mouth, I set the rifle to my right and lift my numbing hands in a surrender motion.

"Very good. Now the pistol, right next to it. Be smart. Two fingers only. Don't want you getting any wild ideas."

I give a nod and make a show of carefully removing my gun and gently tossing it aside.

"Get off me!" Victoria's angry voice sounds through the trees.

"On your feet." Brower motions with his pistol.

As I stand, my legs are spaghetti, barely supporting me. I take in a breath through my nose as my eyes travel over Brower. A bloodstained cloth is wrapped around his bicep, and he's also bleeding above his eye. He wipes the scratch with the back of his free hand, keeping the other steady, with the gun trained on me.

He motions for me to move.

Keeping my eyes on him, I back away from the tree.

"Don't worry, Mrs. Hoffmann. I'm not going to shoot you in the back. When you die, you'll see it coming."

My stomach goes sour.

"Get over there, next to your friend." He motions again with the gun.

Victoria's on her knees in the clearing, her hands laced behind her head. The younger Brower, Declan . . . Mouth . . . whatever his name is, has a gun trained on her.

"On the ground next to her," old man Brower says. "Put your hands behind your head too."

"Sidney's dead." Mouth points to the tall, glassy eyed woman on the ground.

Brower makes a clucking noise with his mouth. "Where's your sister?" He glances around before raising his voice. "Tara? C'mon out here."

My eyes dart to Victoria. Her mouth is tight as she gives a slight shake of her head.

My eyes travel to her hip. Like me, she's been relieved of her sidearm, but her ax is still in place.

I direct my gaze to it and lift my chin. Then I shoot my eyes behind me, toward my ankle. Her eyes go wide as she bites her lip. Again, I look at her hip and then dart my eyes toward Mouth.

"Dad." Mouth motions with his head, his tone hesitant. "Tara's over there."

Lance Brower's eyes travel to where his son indicated. His face goes pale, his eyes filling with tears as he lets out a guttural noise. "Wh-which one of them did this? Who killed my daughter?"

"I didn't see, Dad." Mouth shakes his head. "Let's just kill them both and be done with it. They deserve it anyway for trying to take what's ours. Cattle rustlers and horse thieves deserve to die."

I make a snorting noise. "Cattle rustlers? I'm pretty sure you've got things turned around."

Brower's eyes are still on his dead daughter. His hand twitches.

"Now!" I yell, lowering my right arm as I reach for the baby Glock on my ankle. Out of the corner of my eye, I see Victoria moving with me.

Both Browers also react. My gun is up when a pain rips through my left side. I shoot, emptying the single-stack magazine as I raise my weapon. Brower goes down. My slide clicks open. I toss the gun and then grab for the knife on my belt. I'm on my feet, knife in hand.

"They're down!" Victoria declares.

Lance Brower is a bloody mess. My shots caught him in numerous places, one right between the eyes. Victoria's ax is stuck in Mouth's neck, right at the collarbone. He's making gasping noises. I move to his side and kick his gun out of reach.

"Is he . . ." Victoria asks.

"You . . . you . . . axed me," Mouth mutters in disbelief.

Victoria shrugs out of her backpack and fishes inside for her bandanna.

"It won't help." I shake my head. I kneel next to him and take his hand.

"I'm . . . dying."

"It's not too late . . ." Victoria's voice is gravely. "You can ask God to forgive you. Ask Jesus— "

Mouth puffs out something resembling a laugh. "No thanks." He gasps out a couple of short breaths as he stares at the sky.

"Kimba?" Rey calls to me from an unseen location.

"We're clear."

He steps from the trees, the morning sun picking up the strands of silver in his blond hair. Something flutters deep inside me.

"You're okay?" he asks as he advances toward us, his rifle in low-ready position.

I glance at Victoria, who lifts a shoulder and mumbles, "I guess."

Stumbling to my feet, I take a step toward Rey.

He moves the rifle to the side and opens his arms. The distance between us closes as I melt into him. One strong arm pulls me against him while he drops kisses in my hair and whispers his love for me.

I lift my chin, my eyes meeting his. "I'm sorry. So sorry."

"No, no, it's me. I'm sorry. I should have . . . I haven't done anything right since Nate died. Before he died even. I was a fool. I put us in danger."

"Me too. I wanted this too. I thought it'd be . . ." I shake my head. "Nicole?"

"With Atticus. It's at the mop-up stage, I think. Naomi?"

"I sent her away with Patti and Jameson, to the secondary location."

"Let's go get them and bring everyone home."

I give a nod and step out of his embrace. A wave of pain and nausea comes over me. "Mmm." My hand goes to my side; my fingers feel wet and sticky.

"Kimba? Were you hit?"

"I— " The world tilts as I collapse into my husband's arms.

Chapter 27

Nicole

"Is it over?"

Atticus runs a hand across his scruffy cheek. "Maybe. There hasn't been any shooting for a while. The shots in the distance were the last we heard."

I chew on my top lip. Those shots happened within minutes of the second IED going off. I lost sight of my dad shortly afterward, when he sprinted the rest of the way up the hillside and disappeared.

With the gunfire coming so quickly after the IED detonated, I'm worried. I thought they got out, but now . . .

"What should we do?"

Atticus shakes his head. "Wait."

"For what?" I snap. "My mom might need help *now*."

"Your dad is there. He— "

I raise my hand. "Fine. But I'm not sitting here all day. If it's over, we need to make sure there aren't any injuries. Your brother and Connor, they— "

"I know, Nicole. But until we're certain there isn't someone itching to get us in their crosshairs, we wait."

I shoot him a dirty look.

Several minutes later, Atticus motions toward the line of trees along the river. "See there?"

I scan the area before shaking my head. "I don't see anything."

"There, about halfway— "

"I see it! What is it?"

"A white flag. They're coming out."

"You see them?" Scott calls. "Atticus?"

"I see." Atticus cups his hands around his mouth and yells in a loud, booming voice, "Come on out. Weapons where we can see them."

"You think they can hear you?" I ask, putting my binoculars to my eyes.

Atticus lifts a shoulder before calling out again. The flag gives another wave, then Axel steps out with EJ Martin behind him.

"Axel." Atticus breathes out his brother's name. Soon, the group of seven or eight are out of the woods and in the clearing.

Again, cupping his hands around his mouth, Atticus hollers, "Wait there. Stay covered."

The white flag bounces as the men who are gathered at the edge of the trees stop their movement and step back into the cover of brush.

Atticus turns slightly toward me. "I need to talk to Scott and see if the fence line shooters are eliminated. You ready to move?"

We make our way to the main house where Scott is. "Looks like our men came through." Scott motions with his chin toward Axel and EJ.

"What about the other shooters?" Atticus asks.

"Not sure. I think the ones to the west— "

"Along the fence line?" I ask.

"Yep, those. I think they're done for. But I'm not sure about the guys Hoffmann took off after. Sounded like quite the battle."

My stomach sours again.

"What do we do about Axel and them?" Atticus lifts his chin toward his brother.

"Keep them there until we know? There's too much open space between the trees and here. We still have a shooter, and they'd have no trouble popping a couple off."

"You have a radio?"

"Nope. But I know Brower's channel if you want to give me the one you have. I can call and see if any of the men with EJ has a radio."

Atticus turns to me. "Nicole?"

I thrust the walkie-talkie toward Scott. "It didn't work right earlier."

He fiddles with it a moment before raising it to his mouth. "You got your ears on, Range Rider?"

Seconds later, a deep voice sounds clear and crisp. "Wall to wall and tree top tall, Bulldog."

Atticus and I share a look and shake our heads.

Scott smiles and gives us a wink. "That's a big ten-four. Hang loose for a few minutes while we make sure the coast is clear."

"Aye-firmative. Figured the area wasn't yet secure. Need some help?"

"We're on a party line. Remember the time we went after those elk in Idaho?"

"Meet you there."

Scott again fiddles with the radio. Once he and EJ make contact on a new channel, they come up with a plan for EJ to take Axel and the rest of the group along the river, up and over the hillside to the east, following the same path my dad and Atticus took yesterday.

Atticus tells them to watch for noisemakers, and there's still one IED that hasn't been discharged.

EJ says they'll avoid the ridgeline path and take a lower game trail, which Atticus and Axel both agree is clear of trip hazards.

When they finish the transmission, Scott turns to Atticus. "EJ will make sure things are secured. I'm going to grab one of the others and check out the west side. You cover us?"

"Will do." Atticus looks to me. His eyes drift past me and his head turns.

I snap my head around. "Is it— "

"Victoria and your dad. He's . . ."

"Mom!" I jump up. "He's carrying her."

"Wait!" Atticus orders, grabbing my hand. "We'll go to them, but be smart about it. Scott?"

"Yep." Scott calls out a couple names, ordering his men to cover us. When Scott receives a nod of confirmation, he tells us to go.

We take off up the driveway, toward the road where my parents and Victoria are coming down the steep hill. Mom's in Dad's arms, and Victoria's walking with her rifle up, providing protection.

The pounding of my heart urges my feet to move faster. I force myself to keep the cautious pace Atticus has set. The way Dad's carrying Mom . . . she's hurt. Or worse.

Please, God. Please don't let her be . . . I've been so awful to her. Give me a chance to apologize.

Where's Naomi? Patti and her children? Jameson? My mind screams for answers.

When we're close enough, Dad calls out, "Atticus, can you help me with Kimba?" My dad is breathless and sweating.

Atticus runs the rest of the way, with me by his side.

"What happened?" I ask, taking in my mom's crumpled form and her pale face.

"Gunshot."

I let out a whimper.

"I'm okay," Mom says, sounding anything but. She doesn't even open her eyes. "I'm okay."

I rush to her and reach for her hand, her arm, any part of her.

"Where?"

"Her side," Dad answers.

"You want me to carry Kimba?" Atticus asks.

My dad responds with a weary nod.

I grasp Mom's hand as the transfer happens.

"Nicole." Her voice is ragged, her eye lids flutter. "I'm so glad you're okay."

"I'm fine. W-where's Naomi?"

Victoria shoots me a tight smile. "We sent them to the secondary location. They should be okay. We've stopped your mom's bleeding. Is it . . . safe here?"

"No one's shooting at us at the moment, ma'am," Scott answers. His eyes travel beyond Victoria, scanning the area. "Brower?"

"Dead," Dad answers as he pulls me into a side hug.

With my dad's arm around me and my hand gripping Mom's, tears fill my eyes.

"Let's move. Get Kimba to the house." Dad turns slightly to Scott. "I'm sorry to have to tell you— "

"Tara's dead too." Scott's voice is monotone, his expression unreadable.

My dad bobs his head once. "The son also."

"Sidney? The one who murdered Annie back at Brower's place?"

"Her too."

Scott sighs. "Couldn't be helped. Let's get your wife taken care of. I'd like to . . . Tara deserves a proper burial. They all do."

"Should I go after Naomi?" I ask my dad as we start down the hill.

"I'll go," Victoria says.

Scott looks to my dad. "I'll act as look out for them. I think this is over, but . . ." He raises his hands.

"Better call your friend." Atticus motions to the radio on Scott's belt. "Let them know."

"Will do." Scott nods. He's putting on a brave front, but his face is etched in grief. I'm sure he knew it could end this way, with his fiancée dead—especially considering they were on opposite sides. After a brief conversation on the radio, he motions he's ready.

"What about Connor?" I ask. "Will he . . . you know, with his dad and family dead."

Scott shakes his head. "He knew this could happen. We both did."

My dad gives my arm a squeeze. "Go get your sister. Stay sharp."

After we crest the hill, Axel and his group come into view. He breaks off from the others and makes a beeline for us. "Who's hurt."

"My mom."

"How bad?"

"We're not sure," Victoria says. "Rey's taking her to the house. I'm going after Patti."

"She's at the secondary hideout? Jameson?"

"All of them."

"I'm with you," Axel says. He motions to EJ and his group. "They'll make sure the area is secure. We found Brower."

"And Tara?" Scott asks.

Axel puts a hand on the older man's shoulder. "She's there too."

"Let's get your people situated and get the missus some help. Then I'll come back for them."

"Connor's with them. He's— " Axel shakes his head. "He said he knew it could happen, but he's still . . ."

"Upset." Scott gives a weary nod. "Yeah. Is he alone?"

"Another guy said he'd stay with him."

We near the secondary hideout within a few minutes. Axel calls out to Patti and Jameson as we approach. Soon, my little sister is hugging me and asking for our mom.

"We need to get back to the ranch," I say, looking to Patti. "Mom's been shot. She needs your help."

Chapter 28

Kimba

The room is filled with dim light as a bird sings nearby. I turn slightly but stop when pain rushes through me. Letting out a moan, I puff out several breaths.

"Hey, Kimba." Victoria is by my side. "Don't move too much yet. You need to take it slow."

"Mmm." My arm feels heavy, pinched. It takes me a moment to realize there's an IV stuck in me.

My eyes meet Victoria's. She looks good. Her gray hair, usually stringy and disheveled, is smooth, washed, and brushed as it rests on her shoulders. Even the color is different, brighter. The anxiety lines that have etched her brow and around her mouth for as long as I've known her seem softer.

She gives me a slight smile as she lifts a shoulder. "Brower has—*had*—a lot of medical supplies. Advanced stuff, too, like IVs and surgical kits. You lost a lot of blood."

I take in the room. The full wall of glass, a fireplace . . . Brower's master bedroom. "Why am I here?"

She tilts her head. "Because of the supplies. And there's someone here who knows how to use them. Patti's helping. You're not the only one injured. A couple of EJ's men are, too, and three of Brower's."

"Where's Rey? The children?" I lift my body slightly.

She rests a hand on my arm. "Fine. Everyone's fine. No real injuries, except yours. Your kids are here. Rey too. He hadn't left your side. Even while they were working on you, he was here. It's only been about twenty-minutes since he went to get some rest. I could— "

I let my head sink into the pillow. "No, no. Let him sleep. What time is it?"

"About an hour, hour and a half until sunset. You've been pretty out of it most of the day. Do you . . ." She lifts her eyebrows. "Do you remember?"

I let out a noisy breath. "Do I remember getting shot? The entire day is a blur."

I close my eyes as pieces of it come back to me. Brower and his son planning to execute us for killing Tara and the other woman. Victoria and me making a last-ditch effort to save our lives. Rey appearing. Me collapsing in his arms. I woke up with him carrying me and Nicole asking if I was okay. Then we got back to the houses at the Double D, and they put me in a pickup truck. The ride is like frames of a movie, filled with pain.

Rey was there the entire time, holding my hand and declaring I'd be fine, that they'd take care of me. He loves me.

My eyes fill with tears. I blink rapidly to keep them at bay, to no avail. I move my IV-free arm across my eyes to hide my weakness from Victoria.

She mutters soothing noises as she hands me a handkerchief.

"Oh, Victoria, I've been so awful. So, so awful. To Rey, to all of you."

"No, no. We all understand. Losing Nate like you did . . . we know how much you're grieving." Victoria's eyes fill and she gives a loud sniff. "Losing a loved one is hard. And in today's world, it's . . ." She shakes her head.

I cry for many minutes as Victoria sits next to me, stroking my hair and humming softly. When my tears dissolve into hiccups, she helps me get a drink of water.

"Gently. Only small movements right now."

"Did it hit anything vital?"

"Your injury? Remember how the tent pole stuck in my side the night— " She tilts her head to the side.

"The night of the windstorm, when Nate died."

She responds with a somber nod. "Jameson said the tent pole skewered me. That's pretty much what happened to you. Almost the exact same spot even. The bullet whizzed right through. It took some of you with it, but they think you'll be okay."

"Well, that's good."

"It's a miracle, nothing short of a miracle. God had His hand on you."

"Did He? I'm not sure God even takes much notice of me lately, if He ever did."

She gives me a small smile. "I've felt like that my entire life. Most of it anyway. When I was a child, we went to church. Not regularly, but some. Then, when I married Jon, we went every week. But I never felt like I belonged, not until traveling with all of you and learning about God and His love."

She lifts a shoulder. "Now things are different. I can see it wasn't God not noticing me. He was there, waiting for me to notice Him. Waiting for me to realize my need."

I scrunch up my face. "Until after the EMP, after we settled in Bakerville, God wasn't a part of our lives. Then, suddenly, He was, thanks to Nate." My eyes fill again. "He was the first of us to believe."

We sit in silence for many minutes until I let out a sigh. "I'd always done things on my own. I never even set foot in a church until after I married Rey, after Nicole was born. We only went then because someone invited us to an event. We thought it might be good for Nicole, that maybe we could make amends for some of the things we'd done."

"As spies?" Her mouth twitches as she tries to hold her smile.

A slight laugh escapes me. "*Spies.* It's so funny how people think that. Too many movies and TV shows, I guess. Did you ever watch *Alias* with Jennifer Garner?"

"Yes." She nods vigorously. "Were you— "

"Not even."

"Oh. So, you weren't a spy?"

"I worked in national security, overseas." My eyes meet hers as I raise my eyebrows. "An operations officer. My main objective was to build relationships."

"But something went wrong?" she asks. "That's why you and Doris Snyder had issues when you first arrived in Bakerville?"

"Oh, yes. Something definitely went wrong. Doris was convinced I was a double agent, responsible for the death of . . . of someone she loved. She spearheaded a group that was intent on trying me for treason."

Victoria's mouth goes in an *O* shape. "But you and she . . . things changed."

"Very much so. When we left Bakerville, it was difficult. Doris had become more than a friend. She was family. She's the one who led Nate to Jesus."

"Then I'm forever in her debt."

I crinkle my forehead. "Why's that?"

"She led Nate to Jesus. You became a Christian. You're the reason my sons and I have come to know Christ."

As I look at Victoria, I notice she's different. Not only is her hair combed and she looks more relaxed, but there's also a glow about her. A peace.

"Thank you, Victoria."

"For?" She lifts a hand.

"For being here. For earlier. For helping us survive. For doing what needed to be done."

Her face clouds. "I've never killed anyone before."

I dip my chin. "It's not easy. It *shouldn't* be easy. But it had to be done. They were— "

"Oh, I know. They were going to execute us. I understand it had to happen. But I still feel . . . icky. I've been praying a lot and reading Bible passages Patti suggested. Speaking of Patti, I should tell her you're awake."

"Do you think maybe you could check and make sure Rey isn't up? If he is . . ." I gingerly lift a shoulder.

She gives me a smile. "If he is, I'll make sure he knows you're awake too."

"Thank you." My heart starts beating weird, and an unusual feeling fills my stomach. I hope he's awake. I want to see him. I *need* to see him, to tell him how much I love him and how sorry I am for being so rotten.

A secondary feeling washes over me as I realize he isn't the only one I need to apologize to—Nicole and Naomi, everyone we've been traveling with. Victoria said they all realize I've been grieving, but I still need to make amends. They deserve it.

Is that all?

My hand goes to my chest. No . . . not all. *Please, God. I'm still so angry and sad, so broken over losing Nate. But please, please be patient with me as I sort this out. Help me to know what to do. Help me to stop feeling like this.*

"Hey, sleepy head," Patti's cheerful voice travels through the room.

"Hey. Victoria said you have some fancy stuff to fix me up."

"I'll say." She motions to a man standing next to her. "This is Fedler."

"Ma'am," the man in his late twenties or early thirties says. "Glad to see you're awake. You lost a lot of blood."

I answer with a grim nod.

As Patti and Fedler check my vitals, a rustling noise at the door catches my attention. My stomach does that crazy flip-flop thing again when my eyes meet Rey's.

"Hey." My voice is hoarse and thick.

"Hey." His smile is wide. Gorgeous. He's aged well. With a little silver around his temples and a nearly line-free face, he could be one of those silver fox cover models.

How long has it been since I've looked at him, *really* looked at him? The last several weeks, I've done everything I can to avoid him—avoid his gaze, his hurt expressions. I've shut down and sealed myself off from him, unless it's when I'm snappy.

"Give us just a minute," Patti says. "We'll check her out and then let you two have some time alone."

"Everything okay?" Rey's voice is tinged with anxiety.

"I feel okay," I say quickly. "More with it."

"Your vitals have improved." Patti smiles at me. "The IV's doing its job. We started you on antibiotics."

My eyebrows shoot up. "Antibiotics?"

Her head bobs once. They spend just a few minutes checking me out before Patti gives my hand a squeeze. "Hungry?"

At the mention of food, my stomach responds with a rumble.

She gives a lighthearted laugh. "I'll take that as a yes. I'll be back in a few with something to eat."

After they leave, Rey remains by the door, standing awkwardly and looking nervous. He gives me a timid smile. "I was worried."

"Victoria said you've been sitting with me."

"You look better, have more color."

"Do you want to come in?"

He moves quickly. Instead of sitting in the chair, he kneels at the side of the bed and grasps my hand in his. "Oh, my love. I was so afraid I'd lost you. When you . . ." He sniffs loudly and wipes his eyes. "We'll do what you suggested, find someplace and ride this out. We can stay here, make a life. I can't promise it'll be completely safe. With this world we live in, there're no guarantees."

"I'm so sorry." My voice is hoarse. "I've been so awful to you."

"You were right. Right to blame me. I pushed and pushed— "

"But you didn't. Not really. It was me. It was my insistence we live up to our promises, to the commitment we made to Jennifer and her sons to get them home. And then, when others wanted to join us, it became some noble cause." I squeeze his hand when he opens his mouth to interrupt. "Please, let me finish."

As our eyes meet, he gives me a nod.

I clear my throat. "But that isn't the main thing. It was never you who wanted to help with the rebuilding efforts. It was all me. *Me.* I wanted to make a difference, the kind I never made when I was . . ." I tilt my head. "You know."

"You did good things then, Kimba. The operations you led before— "

I shake my head. "Not enough. And I've used my failure then as an excuse now. Instead of putting our children first, I thought this could be my chance. Because of my arrogance, we lost our son."

"No, love. We lost our son in an accident, something that could've happened anywhere. Even before our world fell apart, children died in car wrecks, house fires, and even tornadoes. Nate's death wasn't your fault." As if reading my mind, he rushes on with, "It's not God's fault either."

My mouth goes in a hard line. "Are you sure?"

"I am. God is intentional in His purpose. Losing Nate doesn't make sense to us now, but I believe it will someday. Thanks to Jesus and the Cross, we know Nate has eternal life. We *will* see him again."

My husband's eyes are glossy with unshed tears. I know the things he is saying, I've heard them preached and spoken, read them in the Bible. Knowing and believing, though, are two different things. Right now, I just want this hole in my heart to heal, for the pain of my loss to lessen. I want my family back.

"Can you forgive me? For the way I've been treating you?"

"I already have, love. The night along the river, when Atticus was reading, I realized then how my bitterness was affecting us—all of us. I begged God to take it from me. I've wanted to talk with you about it, but . . . well, we've been a little busy." The corners of his mouth lift as he waggles his eyebrows.

My stomach does the crazy flip again.

His thumb caresses my hand. "I know you wanted to leave me, to separate."

I suck in my upper lip and shake my head as my eyes fill with tears. "It's not what I want now. I want us back, to be like we used to be. I want Nicole and Naomi to be happy and safe."

"We can stay here. We could make a good life on the ranch. With Brower gone, the people remaining . . . I've spoken with some of them. You'll like them. Remember Brower's cook, Twila? She and the ranch foreman, EJ Martin, they're a couple. They're Christians too. They have some rather— " he scrunches up his nose " —um, *interesting* beliefs. Strong beliefs."

"Like?"

"End times stuff, straight out of Revelation. Mark of the Beast . . . all of it. They think it's started."

"I thought Believers would be raptured before then?"

Rey lifts a shoulder. "I know Chaplain Rick and David Hammer both believed that. But it seems not everyone does. EJ and Twila say they're post-tribbers."

I close my eyes and release a breath. "I hope they're wrong. Aren't Believers supposed to be caught up together with the dead in the clouds? Meet God in the air and be with Him forever?"

"That's right. We will be."

A feeling of dread washes over me. Will I be? Am I truly a Believer? When I accepted Jesus as my Lord and Savior, I did it with my whole heart. For those months we lived with the people of Bakerville, worshipping and studying with them, I was devoted. Even when our community was attacked from within, I never blamed God.

Losing Nate, though . . . how can I truly be a Believer when I have such anger toward God. Had such anger toward my husband? Was my relationship with God trivial at best? Did I not know Him as I thought?

After several beats of silence, Rey gives me a smile. "Anyway, we could make a nice life here. Learn to ride horses, become cowboys."

A burst of laughter escapes me, and the movement causes me to wince.

"Are you okay?" Rey has a panicked look.

"Fine. Just don't make me laugh. You? A cowboy? I mean, you've always looked good in jeans, but . . ." I shake my head. "When we arrived here, that was what I wanted, to stay. But I figured you'd . . . uh, you'd go on to Bozeman."

"Without you? No." A hurt look crosses his face. "You'd force me to go alone? To leave you and the children?"

I drop my gaze. "I'd encourage you to give us some time apart. You could go check on Chad and Beverly, make sure their family is doing well, then we could— "

"Is that still what you want?"

"No." The word comes out with more force than I intend. "No, it's not what I want. Let's talk to the girls and see what they think."

"Nicole wants to go to Billings. She hasn't changed her mind. She's determined to be a part of the rebuilding efforts, even more than before because of the trouble we had with Brower."

I let out a sigh. "Another Brower will pop up. And another and another. Helping with the rebuilding is one thing. Stopping evil is something else."

"I told her that, but she reminded me she'll be eighteen soon."

"Not for two and a half months. We can convince her . . ."

"Really? You think so? She's as stubborn as you are." The smile on his face, combined with the love I hear in his voice, softens his words.

"I think you should kiss me, Mr. Hoffmann."

"Best idea I've heard in a long time, Mrs. Hoffmann."

Chapter 29

Nicole
Sunday, August 9

"Will Mommy really be okay?" Naomi's little face is scrunched in worry.

"Patti says she will," I answer, as we walk toward the Double D. "Plus, you saw her, talked to her. Didn't she look good and sound happy and well?"

My sister lets out an exaggerated sigh. "I guess. But, Nicole, what if— "

"Enough of that." My voice is harsher than I intend. Mimicking her, I let out a sigh of my own. "I'm worried too. But Patti and Fedler seem happy with how she's healing. She just needs more time."

"Her lips looked funny, not pink like they usually do. They just kind of blended into her face."

I purse my own lips as I nod. "She lost a lot of blood. You didn't see her right after. I promise she looks a lot better now than she did then."

After a few steps in silence, Naomi begins to sniffle. When I rest my hand on her shoulder, she goes from sniffling to crying. I bring her to a stop, then kneel down and wrap my arms around my baby sister.

She cries for many minutes as she mutters how scared she is our mom will die. The wetness of my own eyes and the lump in my throat prevent me from doing anything more than making soothing sounds. After several minutes, she straightens and gives a noisy sniffle before saying she's okay now.

As we walk again, her steps seem a little lighter. She even smiles when we hear the warble of a bird.

We stayed at Brower's house last night, sleeping on the floor of his study. Besides Mom, several others were injured and needed to use the beds. Patti's children were with us so their mom could help care for the injured and still feed Trish when needed.

We're going back to the Double D to pack up a few things Patti and her children need. Dad wanted us to wait; he said he'd take us in the pickup as soon as he finished something with EJ Martin. When I told him I needed to stretch my legs, he looked to the hillside, where sentries from EJ's group were keeping watch.

While we believe all of Brower's crew is accounted for, we're still being cautious. Dad agreed to let us go, saying he'll be right behind us. He needs to get Mom's big backpack anyway so she can have a few of her personal items. As an added precaution, I'm carrying a radio. Not that I think it'll be much help, considering how we couldn't get the stupid thing to work during the battle.

Although Brower's spread and the Double D share a fence line, it's almost two miles by road between the driveways. We take our time, enjoying the morning air. There's a light breeze wafting the aroma of the grasses, trees, and the river. My mind also imagines I'm still smelling the gunpowder from yesterday.

Even though I wasn't in the main skirmish, I shot Derek when he and the woman attacked us. Derek isn't doing well. My 9-millimeter round caught bone as it entered, tearing things up and leaving a bloody mess.

Fedler, the guy with the most medical training, was with the attackers along the river. He was loyal to EJ but playing along, waiting for word our group was getting the upper hand. Since he was gone, Derek's early treatment consisted of trying to stop the bleeding. And I'm not really sure how much effort was put into that.

There's some serious animosity between EJ's people and the few left alive who were Team Brower. Patti and Fedler are trying to stabilize all of Brower's men, then they'll be taken to Simms and turned over to whatever law enforcement exists there.

A runner was sent in early this morning to alert the town of what's happened. EJ said that was a risk but necessary. He's sure there're people in Simms who turned a blind eye to what Brower was doing since the man did provide food, though it doesn't sound like he was giving nearly as much to the town as he implied.

EJ's people have already started rebuilding. Not only are they on sentry duty, but they're back to working the cattle and whatever else is needed on a ranch.

Atticus and Axel have reached an agreement with EJ and Scott to team up—not at the peril of losing the Double D this time. EJ says he isn't after Brower's spread. The land belongs to Connor, the only heir, but they'll help him as best they can.

And when things get back to normal, the older men will help with whatever's needed to make things official for both the Double D belonging to Atticus and Axel and Brower's spread to Connor.

As we turn off the paved road and on to the long gravel one, Naomi says, "I thought Dad would've picked us up by now."

"He must've got hung up. You know how everything seems to take longer than we think it will."

"Well, I hope he shows up soon. I don't want to walk back."

"We'll wait for him. Once we get our things together, you can rest."

"You think they'll let me take another shower? It's nice they have hot water. Do you think there will be hot water in Bozeman? In Billings?"

I lift my shoulders. "I don't know, squirt. Things are different everywhere. Brower's solar system and how he had things set up here is perfect, but . . ." I shake my head. "I don't know."

"Dad said he was surprised the lights were still working there, that the EMP didn't affect the solar."

"EMPs are weird. You've seen how most things get fried, but then some things don't. You know there have even been newer cars they were able to get running. I don't really understand how it works, how the EMP seemed to skip over some things and not others."

"Is the way the EMP worked the same as the Bible verse about how we don't know the ways of God?"

I let out a laugh, but at the seriousness on my sister's face, I say, "Um, maybe? I don't think an EMP is the same, though."

"I know that." Her tone is much older than her years. "I mean— " She not only stops talking but stops moving. When I look back at her, she's pale and trembling. Her finger points toward the houses.

I follow her gaze, and my hand goes to my pistol.

"Whoa, whoa." An unkempt man with a huge gun on his hip and a rifle across his back is holding his hands up. "I'm not a threat. I'm here for Atticus . . . um, or Axel."

With my hand still on the grip of my pistol, I step in front of my sister. "Keep your hands up."

"Planned on it, miss." The corners of his mouth lift slightly, moving his bushy mustache and beard. "Do you know where the brothers are?"

"Who are you?"

"Isaiah Millburn, from Simms. Were you traveling with them?"

I raise my eyebrows. "What do you want with them?"

He dips his chin. "I'm here to let them know we found the bear, the one that killed Mrs. Dosen."

My shoulders drop as relief runs through me. "Did you kill it?"

"Nah. No need. It was already dead. Looked a little like . . ." His eyes travel to my side, where Naomi has stepped out from behind me. "Anyway, just wanted to let them know. Thought it might give them a little— " he lifts a shoulder " —closure, maybe?"

I lift my chin. "How'd you get here?"

He motions to the front door of the main house, where a bicycle balances on its kickstand.

Must be nice. We talked about finding bikes for our journey, but there were just too many of us. Now, when we leave here, it's just going to be my family. We'll wait several weeks, or however long Mom needs to heal. She's even willing to continue on now—more than willing. When I spoke with her before leaving Brower's, she sounded almost excited.

She was also very apologetic, telling me over and over how sorry she was for the way she's acted since Nate died. I think coming so close to her own death maybe made her realize what she still has, what we all still have. I miss Nate every minute of every day, and it still hurts to think of him. I don't think the missing will ever leave, but maybe the ache will lessen.

As I meet the man's eyes, he gives me an odd look. "Are you okay?"

When I bob my head to indicate I am, a tear falls from my eye. I quickly swipe at it with the back of my hand. "It's . . . things haven't been easy lately."

His mouth goes into a tight line. "Yeah." After an exceedingly long pause, he asks, "Do you know where Atticus is? I'd like to say hello. Pass on my condolences for— " He shakes his head. "I heard he and Axel are the only ones left. Their parent's, aunt, Asher . . ."

I rapidly blink my eyes. "I don't know, not exactly. He's working the ranch somewhere."

"There he is." Naomi points to two horses cresting a small hill in the pasture. "Axel too. They're together."

The man dips his head. "Thank you. I'll go meet up with them."

As Naomi and I walk to the smaller house, she says, "He seemed nice."

In the distance, the sound of an engine brings a smile to my face. "Sounds like Dad's on his way. Let's hurry and get things together."

Chapter 30

Kimba
Thursday, August 13

"Kimba?" Victoria cheerfully calls from the doorway. "Are you awake?"

"Mmm. Yes." I gently stretch, trying to avoid the pain in my side that accompanies most movement. I'm back in Aunt Nina's little house, having taken over the master bedroom to finish my recovery. They brought me here yesterday, in one of the pickup trucks driving at the speed I'd normally walk. It was still grueling.

"Scott's here. He asked to see you. Is that okay?"

"Uh, yeah. But first . . ." I lower my voice. "I'm a mess. Grab me a brush?" I slowly scoot up as Victoria steps into the room.

She rushes to my side, helping me adjust the pillows. "You look fine. The braid is still secure. No reason to undo it. Besides, Scott knows you were shot."

I tilt my head in agreement. "Okay. I just hope he doesn't get too close. I stink."

"How about I help you with that after Scott leaves?"

I give her a nod and let her know she can send him in. It's several minutes from the time she exits the room until Scott appears. So long, I'm starting to wonder if he changed his mind.

"Hello, Kim . . . um, Kimba?"

"Kimba," I agree with a nod. "Kim is . . . well, someone I hope we never see again."

He gives me an uncomfortable smile. "I knew you were more than you seemed. Rey too. All of you really. When you first showed up, I thought this might happen."

My brow crinkles. "I'm sorry for your loss. Tara . . . I know— "

He raises a hand. "Obviously, I wish things would've ended differently. I thought Tara was safe, tied up. I thought, once it was over, she'd . . ." He shakes his head. "You may be wondering why I was with her."

I lift a shoulder. "I'll admit, the thought crossed my mind. But I realize we can't help who we love." I think about a short-term boyfriend I had in the past, during my days in government service. I thought I was in love with him, but when I learned what he was truly like . . . an involuntary shudder runs through my body.

"You cold?" Scott moves toward a chair with a throw blanket on it.

"No, no." I wave him away. "I'm fine."

He dips his chin in agreement. "Anyway, Tara was always a flirt. When things were normal, she'd ride over here, wearing tight Wranglers and . . . it doesn't matter. I think she had a thing for Atticus then. Or maybe Asher. She wasn't overly particular who paid attention to her." A look of hurt quickly crosses his face.

"When things fell apart, she didn't waste much time before turning her attention to me. She was scared. Lonely. I was scared, even lonelier, and flattered. Tara was beautiful. Vibrant. Young."

I resist the urge to point out she was too young. Scott must be in his thirties. His sun-weathered face adds to his age, but I'm sure he's at least a decade older than Tara was.

He gazes out the window. "Connor was right, you know. Tara wasn't going to marry me. We would've ended almost as soon as it started if she didn't need the house—the Double D ranch house—as an escape from her dad. She may have acted the part of daddy's little girl, but she secretly hated him."

Scott shakes his head. "Not really secretly. Everyone knew about her temper tantrums. Twila had tried to help her. She'd been with them since before they moved here, when Mrs. Brower was still alive. Tara was a brat, even then."

Giving him a sad smile, I can't help but wonder why he's here, why he's telling me this. I briefly saw him after the shootout. I apologized for killing Tara—no matter that it wasn't likely my bullet that ended her life. Whether it was Victoria or me, the end result is the same. He'd said he knew we were given no choice in the matter.

Scott spends several more minutes almost reminiscing about Tara and how she was both before and after the EMP. He not only shares about her bratty ways but also a few cute stories.

I smile and nod when appropriate, feeling badly for him. While I can accept that we did what we had to do, I understand he's still grieving.

It especially hits home when he says, "I guess I thought I could change her. There were good parts to her. She was so sweet with the horses and cattle, the barn cats. She was almost like a little girl when she was around the animals. I thought that showed the good in her and I could maybe bring that part out, nurture it so she was good to people—to me—in the same way. I really thought . . ." He lets out a sigh.

"Doesn't matter. Anyway, you must be wondering why I'm droning on about Tara." He gives me a pointed look.

The corners of my mouth lift slightly. "The thought had crossed my mind. But I get it. Talking about those we loved and lost, it helps."

He nods. "Like your little boy. I didn't know. You and Rey pretended like you didn't have children. I suspected, with the resemblance of the girls, but I had no idea about your son. I'm terribly sorry for your loss."

A lump forms in my throat, and I dip my chin. My voice comes out thick. "Thank you. It's not easy. Grief . . . give yourself time, Scott. Remember all the good things about Tara and allow yourself to feel."

"I will. I am. Anyway, I've been talking with EJ and Twila. I feel bad about my part in this whole thing, about how maybe I could've stopped it. And I especially feel bad about you getting shot and the children being in danger. I was too loose lipped the night it all went down. I knew where they'd stashed you, and I made a point of giving away that information—loudly.

"I didn't . . . at the time, I had no idea Tara, Sidney, and Derek had escaped. They must have been lurking nearby, listening as we put our plans together. Tara wasted no time going to Lance with what she knew. It's my fault you're lying here."

I raise a hand. "It isn't your fault, Scott. You had no way of knowing how this would all play out. You stepped up when it mattered. Of course, the way Rey tells it, you scared them all half to death by meeting them at the back door like that. How'd you know?"

"Fedler."

"Fedler? The medic?"

He raises his brows. "He and his buddy were watching you that day. When they left, Fedler caught a glimpse of Atticus and knew you all were on to them."

I shake my head. "And he just walked away?"

Scrunching up his face, Scott gives a nod. "Fedler knew about the two who replaced them. Those two were killers. And worse. Atticus felt bad about taking the guy's life the way he did, but he shouldn't. The way they were wasn't a secret. A few of the others, too, but they're all dead now. The ones like Fedler, who were loyal to EJ, they knew what was happening and kept their heads down.

"Most of them are good men that found their way here and took up Brower on his promise of food and lodging for ranch hands. *Ranch hands.* Not hired killers. A couple of them are struggling with the things they've done. Reminds me a little about this book I read about a police battalion during the Holocaust. They were just regular guys, then they became killers."

"I read that too. *Ordinary Men.* That was part of the title. I don't remember the rest of it. But you're right. They were average middle-aged guys. Working class. They turned into mass murderers. Not all of them, some did their best to avoid the killing, but I think that was the minority."

"Right. EJ had Fedler, and a few others like him, who managed to avoid the worst of it. Of course, EJ did too. Brower knew better than to even ask EJ to participate. At the other end of the spectrum were the cold-blooded killers, the ones who found they enjoyed it. Brower had a handful of them. The two Atticus and your husband capped were in that group."

I nod, remembering the soulless eyes of the man in the red ballcap.

"But most did what they did because they looked at it like their job. That's what a few of the guys here did. They're the ones having trouble, looking for ways to make amends. Not sure they'll find it."

I purse my lips. I know about people doing their jobs. I was there once—a robot doing what I was ordered. I'd like to think I was always on the side of right, but was I? Even when Rey and I started our own gig, there were sometimes questions in my mind as to who the good guy was and whether they were the ones employing us.

"It happens, I guess," Scott continues, inclining his head. "Probably more often than we think. People get in a group, get brave, and do things they'd never think of doing on their own. I never participated in Brower's . . . stuff. But I willingly turned a blind eye. I don't think the guys feeling bad will be the end of it either."

"Meaning?"

"Meaning, I expect we'll see fallout."

The question must be written on my face.

He raises both hands. "I don't know for certain. I just think Lance caused enough damage someone might show up looking for revenge. Or on the flip side, his cohorts might decide what we've done here isn't okay."

"Cohorts? You mean the supporters from Simms? The ones he had deals with for food and supplies?"

"Yup. Those. And others. You hear about Isaiah Millburn showing up the other day?"

I search my memory for the name, then lift a shoulder.

"He came to tell Atticus and Axel about finding the bear dead and to give his condolences. But I also think he was making sure the boys knew that there may be trouble."

"Rey knows about this?"

"He and EJ both."

Closing my eyes, I let out a slow breath through my nose. Rey didn't say anything to me about this. Either he doesn't think it's a threat or he's keeping me out of the loop. I aim to find out which it is.

"Well, I've yacked your ear off long enough. Please, I do hope you'll accept— "

I raise a hand. "You have nothing to apologize for. I knew what may happen. I'll be . . ." I clear my throat. "I'll pray for you as you work through your grief over Tara." Telling Scott I'll pray for him feels almost foreign. But it also feels right. Truthful.

"Thank you. I appreciate it. Pray for Connor too. He knew what might happen, but it still weighs heavy on him, losing his entire family like that. He knows how they were, but like me seeing the good in Tara, he knew the good parts about them. There may not have been a lot of love in that family, not after Connor's mom died, but I think he always *hoped* it could be fixed, that somehow he could make his dad proud. Now that opportunity's gone."

Vowing to include Connor in my petitions to God, Scott says his goodbyes. I lean back on my pillow and replay the conversation. Scott seemed to be airing a guilty conscience. Was it strictly what he said? Did he feel badly about giving away our position in the fort? I'd like to take him at face value, take this as nothing more than a step toward his own healing.

I certainly hope that's the case.

Chapter 31

Nicole
Sunday, August 23

"Let's raise our glasses to the bride and groom." Scott tilts his champagne flute toward EJ and Twila.

Even though Lance Brower still owned a well-stocked wine cellar and had plenty of homemade spirits, this is a temperance reception. The flutes are filled with flavored waters.

Half a dozen fancy glass beverage dispensers were lined up on a skirted table, each filled with ice water—ice water! A chest freezer in the basement, powered by solar, gave us this long-forgotten treat. Each dispenser had a different fruit, herb, or vegetable floating among the ice. I chose raspberry water, Naomi picked strawberry, Dad took basil, and Mom got cucumber.

Mom being here and well enough to lift a glass in toast and laugh with us is amazing. Although I told my sister Mom would be fine, reassuring her constantly, I was still scared. The way she looked when Dad was carrying her back to the Double D—pale, limp, lifeless . . .

But now here she is. She looks better than she has in months. Not just better than since she was shot, but better since Nate died. The lines that had taken over her face have lessened. She's even putting on a little weight, thanks to not walking daily and the fare from the large gardens and culled cattle. Her eyes are still sad, just like the rest of us, but not nearly as desperate looking.

I know things will never be the same as they were before, when our family was complete, but I can feel us healing—becoming something new.

Another week of rest and Fedler says Mom should be up for traveling. There's a bit of the old excitement we had months ago when still living at the lodge and planning our journey. While most everyone was excited to return home or to family, for us it was an adventure. A way to make our mark in history.

It's different now, especially for Mom. Dad too, I suspect. But Mom has stopped talking about making a difference for our country and now talks about helping people. She's sure our longtime friends Chad and Beverly are doing well, and she's looking forward to visiting with them.

My eyes travel to Atticus and Axel. They're in a group that includes Jameson and Brett. I'll miss them when we leave. Even Jameson, who was a thorn in my side for most of our journey.

As he stands next to his older brother, I can see the changes in him. Not just physical, though he has grown several inches since we started, but in his demeanor. He's no longer the brat he once was. Sure, he still has his moments and likes to tease, but it's not the same. Where before his teasing seemed full of malice, now he's more lighthearted and . . . I can't even explain it.

Jameson laughs at something someone says and then turns to Connor Brower.

After the death of his dad and siblings, Connor struggled. Even with all the bad stuff they did, they were still his family.

I didn't attend, but there was a small burial service for everyone lost in the battle. The top of a hillside across the road was designated as the graveyard. My eyes travel to the spot, not far from where my dad and us hid that night while waiting to attack Brower and end the conflict.

Catching movement out of the corner of my eye, my breath catches. There're half a dozen people on horseback. One of the women from Brower's former household staff let's out a cry and points toward them.

"Dad?" I ask, grabbing Naomi's hand.

"How'd they get past our guard?" Mom asks.

"Don't know." Dad shakes his head. "Nicole, take your sister to the other side of the corral and use the barn for cover. If things go bad, get to the river. Meet at the fallback position your mom used—the one Patti was at. Kimba?"

"I . . ." She shakes her head, her hand going to her injured side. "I'll stay with you. Where's Patti and Victoria?"

"Kimba!" Patti calls from near where Atticus and his group were talking. Even with a child on each hip, she still moves quickly.

"Go to her," Mom says. "Tell her the plan. She'll need your help."

"But— " I swallow the lump in my throat. "Why are they just riding in all calm?"

"We'll be sure and find out." Mom dips her head. "Go to Patti."

Naomi and I sprint to our friend. Victoria reaches her seconds before us, opening her arms to take LJ. Jameson and Brett are with their mom.

People are running everywhere. A group, which includes EJ and Scott, are at one of the pickups. The Dosen brothers and several others are at the horses, saddling them. Many people pull out rifles and take defensive positions. Mom and Dad, armed only with their pistols, move much slower than Mom would've before she was shot.

Dad calls out to EJ and asks them to wait for them.

"What do we do?" Victoria asks.

"Dad said to move to the other side of the corral and be ready to go to the river if things go bad."

"Who are they?" Jameson asks. "Why are they coming up the road? If they were here to . . ." He shakes his head. "Wouldn't they sneak?"

"They could be a diversion." Brett juts his chin in their direction. "Let's go. Atticus told Jameson and me to stay with you."

I urge Naomi to hurry. We need to be behind cover before things go pear-shaped. On the other side of the barn, I'm surprised to find Twila—the bride—and several of her household staff.

Twila's eyes are filled with fear and her mouth is turned down at the corners, but she gives my group a curt nod. "Some wedding party."

One of the women beside her pats her arm. "We'll have great stories to tell when this turns out to be nothing."

"I pray so."

"That's what we need to do." Patti motions to the women. "Pray."

From the edge of the barn, Brett says he'll keep watch.

I move to join him when Victoria takes my hand. "Prayer first."

Allowing only a brief moment for the group to settle, I'm surprised when Victoria's voice rings out strong and clear. She praises God for who He is and the love He gives us. She thanks Him for saving her from herself and asks that He take us all in His mighty arms and keep us safe.

A lump forms in my throat as her heartfelt words wash over me. She's no longer the woman she once was. God's promise to make us a new creation in Christ has surely come true as far as Victoria Dawson is concerned. The old is gone and the new is here, standing strong before us.

After a hearty round of amens for the short prayer, I wipe my eyes and then tell Naomi to stay with Victoria and Patti while Jameson and I move toward Brett.

"What's happening?" I ask.

"Looks like . . . I think they're talking."

I kneel on one knee so I can get a peek without Brett's head being in my way. He's right. The intruders have stopped, as have our group in the pickup and on horseback, allowing a good hundred yards between them.

I can make out my dad standing on one side of the truck and EJ Martin on the other. I don't see my mom. Axel and Atticus are both atop their horses. I feel my shoulders drop in relief.

"We're okay?" Jameson's voice cracks. He clears his throat. "I mean, it's not an attack, right?"

"Let's just wait," Brett answers. "Be ready to move . . . but I think we might be okay."

Glancing over my shoulder, I meet Naomi's wide eyes and give her a small smile.

It's many minutes before the two groups move closer together. Everyone is off their horses and there are handshakes all around.

I don't find out until later that the eastern guard had used the radio to announce a group from Simms was arriving. The western guard had heard and acknowledged the transmission, but for some reason the ranch guard didn't receive it. Knowing how awful their radios work, I'm not surprised. It's a definite weakness in their security they need to fix.

The four men and two women from Simms knew about the wedding from when EJ and Twila were in town yesterday, being married by the preacher. They had no idea there was a party today but wanted to bring a few gifts of congratulations.

Isaiah Millburn, the young man who'd unintentionally frightened Naomi and I the day after the battle, is among the visitors. He tilts his hat at me and delivers a brilliant smile before turning back to visit with Axel, Atticus, and Connor.

Part of me finds it amusing Isaiah has once again scared the daylights out of me. The other part of me admires his kind smile. I also notice he's cleaned up considerably since the last time I saw him. His beard is trimmed, and his hair is clean—or at least not as greasy and unkempt. He's even wearing clean clothes. If we were staying here . . .

I shake the thought from my head. We're not staying. We're moving on, on to Bozeman and then to Billings. After that, we might go home to Denver. Or maybe I'll join the military. I'll be eighteen in a few months, and I know they're looking for volunteers, having formed several new units. They even call those units the Volunteer Units.

Dad says he doesn't think they're real military with the same benefits, but I'm not sure I care. Before, I wanted to stay with my family as we made our mark together. Now, like my mom, I want less to be a part of history and more a part of helping individuals, making a difference in people's lives. The Volunteer Unit just may be the best place for me to do so.

Chapter 32

Kimba
Monday, August 31

"You're sure you're ready? It's only been three weeks since you were shot." Victoria's eyes meet mine as she slightly releases me from the hug. "You could stay a few more days and heal up a little more."

I give her a wobbly smile as my eyes fill. "I'm doing good. And we'll take it easy."

She lets out a noisy breath as she blinks her damp eyes. "I'll miss you, Kimba. All of you."

In today's world, saying goodbye feels permanent. Maybe the public transports will be safe and convenient, making traveling for pleasure a reality again in the future.

And with the return of mail service, we can exchange letters. Nicole's already written letters to the Monroes, Rochelle Bennet, and Tamra Nicholson. Rey, Naomi, and I each added our own short hellos. I should've written more, but finding the words was difficult. Maybe, if these reach them and we receive return letters, then I can take up my own correspondence.

Nicole's hoping there will be a mail drop near where we get on the bus to Butte. In the letter, she told them we're going to Bozeman, but only for a short while. She'll write again once we're settled in Billings to tell them how to reach us.

I'm of the mind that while these letters may reach them—at least the Monroes and Tamra Nicholson, since they're settled in small areas—finding us in a small city like Billings will be more of a challenge.

As far as Rochelle Bennet, we don't know where she is. Did she find her son and make it back to Bakerville? Nicole's sending the letter there, assuming she has. She also wrote to Doris Snyder in Bakerville. I know Doris and her husband will be brokenhearted when they learn about Nate's death.

Writing the letters was almost therapeutic for Nicole, telling of our losses and experiences. Even if she never mails them or they never receive them, I'm glad she did it.

We continue rounds of hugs, telling everyone goodbye. During the last few weeks, since Brower and his threat was eliminated, the two ranches have come together as one.

Connor Brower, still grieving over the loss of his family and his part in it, is relying on EJ Martin and his wise guidance.

The Dosen boys, filled with their own grief, are running the Double D. There was little time for any of us to mourn Jennifer's loss. As soon as we arrived, we were plunged into the conflict with Brower.

I'm glad Victoria and Patti are here. They'll be a help to them. Especially Axel, who still seems more angry than sad. When he found out the bear was dead, it didn't give him the closure he thought it would.

Axel and Atticus have moved into the main house. Scott is back in the caretaker's cabin, while both Jameson and Brett live in the bunkhouse. Victoria, Patti, and the babies will stay in Nina's place. Truthfully, I'll be surprised if Patti leaves in the spring. They could make a good life here on the Double D.

"Ready?" Rey reaches for my hand.

I take his with a smile. While there are still some sore spots between us, we're working on reconnecting, on communicating. I've come to realize how misplaced most of my anger was. While I'm still hurting from losing Nate, Rey isn't to blame. And a part of me has also come to realize God is not to blame. When he died, I was so angry. So hurt. I lashed out at everyone.

During the time I've been healing from my gunshot wound, I've also come to realize what a hypocrite I was. When I first became a Christian, I was so excited, so passionate. I was convinced I knew everything.

I'm almost embarrassed when I think about how preachy I could be in those early days. Tamra Nicholson had questions about God, and instead of calmly answering them, I was a zealot and practically hit her over the head with my Bible to convince her how much she needed God.

But when tragedy struck, when Nate died, my enthusiasm wasn't enough. My relationship with God was shallow, tenuous. I was a baby

Christian, being fed and guided by those in Bakerville who knew the scriptures, knew God.

When we ventured out on our own, we had Jennifer, who was strong in her walk with Christ. But even Jennifer faltered. When we first met Patti, we saw a different side of Jennifer. A side of prejudice. Before her death, she seemed to overcome it, to take her troubles to God and to grow in Christ. Jennifer made amends.

For me, when I lost Nate, I didn't have a reservoir of inner strength fed by God to draw from. Instead, I distanced myself from Him. From my husband. Even from my daughters.

Now I'm trying to find myself again, find the person I was becoming. I'm praying with Rey and the others—even reading the Bible. Things are different this time, though. Where before I felt a burning and longing to show people just how good of a Christian I am, now I'm almost embarrassed. Not of Christ, but of myself. Of my behavior.

As we say our final goodbyes to our friends, I'm almost glad to be leaving them. As much as I'll miss them, I'm looking forward to a fresh start, being with new people who won't know how awful I've been. Victoria and Patti were very gracious when I apologized for being so snippy and difficult. Both said they understood, and I'm sure they did, having each been recently widowed. But I'm still ashamed.

"What are you thinking about?" Rey asks as we walk down the driveway.

I shake my head. "How much I'm going to miss sleeping in a real bed."

He snorts out a laugh. "Me too."

We walk a few more steps in silence before I drop my shoulders. "That's not really what I was thinking."

"Oh?"

When I look at Rey, I see two more pairs of eyes trained on me. My daughters are also waiting for my admission. I clear my throat. "I was thinking about God and second chances."

Rey and Naomi smile, while Nicole furrows her brow.

"I was just . . . I was thinking . . ." I take in a deep breath. "I was thinking how patient He's been with me. How patient all of you have been. Thank you for that."

I catch a slight eye roll from Nicole before she focuses on the ground ahead of us. Rey squeezes my hand, while Naomi says, "I'm glad you feel better and are ready to walk. Nicole said, if we stay at the Double D much longer, we're gonna get stuck in a snowstorm."

Nicole shoots her sister a look.

With a happy laugh, I nod my agreement. "Indeed. I was ready to get moving too."

"We're taking it easy today," Rey reminds me for the umpteenth time. "As soon as you need to stop, we will."

As we turn the corner from the gravel driveway on to the paved road, I catch sight of our shadows—Rey and me, hand in hand, with the girls by our sides, each of us carrying a restocked backpack, thanks to the Dosen boys and Connor Brower going out of their way to make sure we have what we need: more food, medical supplies, batteries, so many things.

The 9-millimeters on Nicole's, Rey's, and my hips are prominent in our outline but pale in comparison to the slinged long guns. Rey's carrying the AR-15, Nicole the shotgun, and I have my .308. I'm also carrying the backpack Leanne Monroe gave us, which has a sling sewn into it. Tucked in the sling is the .22 Victoria was using when we were in the hideout—the same light rifle Nate used to carry.

The Dosen boys also made sure we had a new supply of ammo. Their dad's reloading station, which had only been mildly pilfered since the collapse, gives them a fresh supply of ammo. We still have a small supply of shells for the 12 gauge, including double aught buck, slugs, and a couple of different bird loads. And Connor gave us a small box of .22 ammo as a going away gift.

Though we hope not to need them, I feel a measure of comfort leaving here well-armed. Just like when we left the ski lodge back in March, we don't know what our future holds. Even so, I can't help but smile. *Thank you, God. Thank you for helping us through the dark times. Thank you for not giving up on me.*

The adventure continues in *Enduring Havoc: Montana Mayhem Book 6*, coming available September 2022.

In the final leg of their journey, Kimba and her family head to Bozeman, Montana, to check on their longtime friends, Chad and Bev. But what they find isn't what they expected.

Also by Millie Copper

Montana Mayhem Series

Unending Havoc: Montana Mayhem Book 1

Ruthless Havoc: Montana Mayhem Book 2

Merciless Havoc: Montana Mayhem Book 3

Cruel Havoc: Montana Mayhem Book 4

Havoc in Wyoming Series

Wyoming Refuge: A Havoc in Wyoming Prequel

Havoc in Wyoming: Part 1, Caldwell's Homestead

Havoc in Wyoming: Part 2, Katie's Journey

Havoc in Wyoming: Part 3, Mollie's Quest

Havoc Begins: A Havoc in Wyoming Story (Part 3.5)

Havoc in Wyoming: Part 4, Shields and Ramparts

Havoc in Wyoming: Part 5, Fowler's Snare

Havoc Rises: A Havoc in Wyoming Story (Part 5.5)

Havoc in Wyoming: Part 6, Pestilence in the Darkness

Christmas on the Mountain: A Havoc in Wyoming Novella

Havoc Peaks: A Havoc in Wyoming Story (Part 6.5)

Havoc in Wyoming: Part 7, My Refuge and Fortress

Nonfiction Books

Sourdough for Your Food Storage: Add Nutrition and Variety to Your Baked Goods

Sprouts for Your Food Storage: Add Nutrition and Variety to Your Diet

Stock the Real Food Pantry: A Handbook for Making the Most of Your Pantry

Design a Dish: Save Your Food Dollars

Real Food Hits the Road: Budget Friendly Tips, Ideas, and Recipes for Enjoying Real Food Away from Home

Stretchy Beans: Nutritious, Economical Meals the Easy Way

Find these titles on Amazon:
www.amazon.com/author/milliecopper

Acknowledgments

Thanks to:

Ameryn Tucker, my editor, beta reader, and daughter wrapped in one. I had a story I wanted to tell, and Ameryn encouraged me and helped me bring it to life.

Dee from Dauntless Cover Design.

My husband, who gave me the time and space I needed to complete this dream and was very patient as I'd tell him the same plot ideas over and over and over.

Three more daughters and a young son, who willingly listen to me drone on and on about story lines and ideas while encouraging me to "keep going."

My amazing Beta Readers! Thanks to Barbara, Becky, Judy, Linda, Tammy, Tonya, and Tracy for your help in creating the final story. Your insights and abilities to see the things I miss are very much appreciated! And a special thank you to Tim, specialist in all things that go boom, for always answering my questions and pointing out things I wouldn't even think about.

And to you, my readers, for spending your time with our band of weary travelers. If you have five minutes, you'd make this writer very happy if you could leave a review. I appreciate you!

About the Author

Millie Copper, writer of Cozy Apocalyptic Fiction, was born in Nebraska but never lived there. Her parents fully embraced wanderlust and moved regularly, giving her an advantage of being from nowhere and everywhere.

As an adult, Millie is fully rooted in a solar-powered home in the wilds of Wyoming with her husband and young son, milking ornery goats and tending chickens on their small homestead. In their free time, they escape to the mountains for a hike or laze along the bank of the river to catch their dinner. Four adult daughters, three sons-in-law, and three grandchildren round out the family.

Since 2009, Millie has authored articles on traditional foods, alternative health, homesteading, and preparedness-many times all within the same piece. Millie has penned five nonfiction, traditional food focused books, sharing how, with a little creativity, anyone can transition to a real foods diet without overwhelming their food budget.

The twelve-installment *Havoc in Wyoming* Christian Post-Apocalyptic fiction series uses her homesteading, off-the-grid, and preparedness lifestyle as a guide. The adventure continues with the newly released *Montana Mayhem* series.

Find Millie at www.MillieCopper.com
Facebook: www.facebook.com/MillieCopperAuthor/
Amazon: www.amazon.com/author/milliecopper
BookBub: https://www.bookbub.com/authors/millie-copper